JUST BILL

A NOVEL
BY
BARRY KNISTER

Gold Mountain Press

Just Bill is a work of fiction.
Any similarity of characters to persons
living or dead is coincidental.

Also by Barry Knister: *THE DATING SERVICE*

©2008 Barry Knister.
Published by Gold Mountain Press.
All rights reserved.
Printed in the United States of America.

Book design by TCA Graphics.
Cover photo courtesy of Georgia Nelson.

ISBN: 978-0-9821588-0-7

Returned to the animal shelter, he resumes a life of sordid, empty days. Dogs come and go. Filling the hours, a welter of sensory overload gives way to boredom. Harsh Florida sun hangs all day in front of his crate; at night, shards of lightning stab down through the skylight. Being brought back this way and again confined, he has trouble eating. In four days he loses two pounds.

Then, on the fifth day he is let out in the morning with others, in the fenced yard. Hot and humid, the air is something to push through. By noon the sky has darkened, and by two the trees bordering the adjacent barns rattle and sway. Dust whips through the yard. A plastic bucket flies against the stucco wall, then a lawn chair. One of the animal-shelter staff is now crossing from the sheds where public works equipment is stored. Hunched and facing away, she is holding on to her broad Smokey-the-Bear hat. As she nears the gate, her phone rings. She unclips it from her belt and starts talking, holding her hat, working to open the gate. The hat blows off. Still talking, she turns and starts chasing it, back toward the sheds. The hat whips and bounces.

The gate bangs open.

—Come on.

The German shepherd is already outside. Skillfully mastering his injured leg, he starts loping away. It's wrong, the dog thinks, watching. Running away is a bad thing you get scolded for, even hit on the nose with newspaper. He watches other dogs scuttle out, the woman still chasing her hat.

He chooses, and runs. Digging his hindquarters and racing for the gate, he bangs a Weimaraner on the way—and then he's out, racing to catch the shepherd. It's easy to do, the shepherd hobbled. But he is now loping in a steady, altered three-legged canter, clear of purpose. The dog reaches him. The message coming to him from the shepherd has to do with distance, the need to leave the shelter behind. In back of them he hears shouting, faint in the wind. Ahead, a fallen palm frond whisks across the road. In seconds they reach the highway. They run west, side by side on the shoulder.

—Just run, the shepherd signals. —Don't look back. Run.

They do, together. He paces himself to match the slower dog. Everything now is wind. Everywhere leaves and torn seeds fly at them—they're running directly into the first hours of a storm that has brewed for days in the Caribbean. Now rain falls in sheets. It doesn't start small, there's no light pattering first, no slow build. It's thrown, pitched and dumped on all beneath. On the right the hot asphalt steams. Traffic barrels past, lashing the two dogs with waves. Horns bray. Headlights and fog lamps seem to charge all at once through the curtain, whipping past.

How far? A mile? All there is to know lives in his big legs and chest, energy and instinct. And the shepherd. Would he have run without him? Either way he has made another choice on another road, this one in Florida, in hurricane season, dodging a branch torn from a cabbage palm.

And in the clatter and steam of it, the slashing spray of passing cars— something registers. He knows this place. In his brain, narrow but deep in terms of sound and smell, he is certain. Ahead, lights are flashing. Some cars have pulled off the road. Nearing them, he leads the shepherd, picking up more clearly the scent and certainty that he is right.

—This is good, he barks. —On the other side. I know what this is.

No time or need to think. He cuts right and dashes over asphalt. This is where he lives, this is the mister and missus, the pool and rugs, the bed to be under in storms like this. Tires skid, a horn blows. Still it blares. On the wide median he stops. The shepherd isn't with him. He whines and barks, a surprise even to those hard pressed to get where they need to be in such a storm. For a moment, distracted from worry about their cars and houses, they point at him. Slowing, they inch along the right lane as others still race in the left, many talking on cell phones, telling one more detail from this squall-soaked day on Davis Boulevard, telling the person on the other end about some crazy dog out on the median, maybe a Labrador retriever, a big one barking his damn head off in all this weather.

If this afternoon the dog's owner were traveling in one of the passing cars, deafened by drumming on roof and hood and slowed by the storm, so that he all at once saw what was there, on the median, it would break his heart. With furious drivers honking and yelling, he would stop his car, get out and call to his dog.

But he isn't there. And what's happening on Davis Boulevard is months away. Right now it's late spring, with things as they should be.

JUST BILL

For Barbara

The Floozy

"It's not your fault, it's my fault. Don't you see, Hotsie? God, out buying pots..."

On the grass behind the Gilmores' pool enclosure, four dogs watch as Glenda Gilmore again breaks down. She's on the couch in her living room, dressed in a black leotard and shorts. "My fault, my fault—" She shakes her head, pounding her knees. As he has for twenty minutes, Hotspur sits opposite, bolt upright on Cliff Gilmore's BarcaLounger. His black coat glistens under track lighting, chest and muzzle pure white. As if to console Glenda, the border collie raises a paw.

—She keeps talking about a sale, Emma says. —She was shopping when it happened.

—Sale?

Emma, a miniature poodle, glances at Chiffon lying next to her on the grass. Chiffon is a bichon frise. The look of separation anxiety on her face comes any time something disturbs her lapdog life. Emma turns back. —More tears, she says. —'All my fault, should have been here.'

—Fault?

The sun is setting. Again the poodle turns, this time to look out on the golf course. Everything is just now turning pink, the lawn and white sand traps, the blank row of condos to the west. Late-afternoon players are all in now, the last golf cart back in the shed. Here and there the eleventh fairway is traced by wide tire tracks. On the far side, the coming of darkness is marked by the bone-white trunks of melaleuca trees. Birdcalls in the upper branches mingle with Glenda Gilmore's crying. *Ditzy*, Emma thinks. She doesn't know what it means, but often hears the word used with *Glenda Gilmore*. And *floozy*.

—She is a good missus.

For emphasis, Bill lowers his big body to the grass. He settles with paws extended and head erect, intent on the Gilmore living room. —She likes to walk. She likes playing Frisbee. She goes with her mister when he takes Hotspur to the beach. Glenda is a good missus.

Emma looks again to the open doorwall. Still motionless, Hotspur has not taken his eyes off the crying woman. He can't, of course, he's a border collie. But Glenda Gilmore won't see it that way. To her, Hotspur's unwavering gaze means he's paying attention, being sympathetic. That's why she loves him so much tonight, confiding in him, apologizing, confessing. They're more or less all like that, even Emma's own mistress, Madame.

—Stop crying, Luger growls. —People get old, people die. Geddagrip.

The toy schnauzer on Emma's left shakes his head free of gnats. *Geddagrip* is something his mister says all the time.

—I feel sorry, Chiffon whines. —Crying is unhappy. When my missus cries, I cry too. She's old, she says so. Her mister died and she cries. It's sad.

—Feel sorry for Hotspur, Emma says. —He has to keep sitting there.

—Hotsie is a dog.

—So are you.

—No. I'm Babycakes. Snookums. Love muffin.

She's old, it's sad. Except "old" does not apply to Glenda Gilmore. Not at Donegal Golf and Country Club. Before she married Cliff and came here, she was a Lands' End model. That's why the other club wives call her a floozy.

Rising now with the Kleenex box, she disappears behind half-closed vertical blinds. At last Hotspur is free to look out. He's heard and smelled the other dogs all this time, and wants to run out through the open doorwall to greet them. But he must now weigh this impulse against his sense of duty. It's bred into him, like his border-collie stare. Finally deciding, he hops down and trots after his mistress.

—People die, Luger says again. —They live, they die.

—You told us, Emma says.

—Work hard, play hard, die. No crying.

—You told us.

—Work hard, play hard—

She barks at him. The single, harsh report echoes out into the darkness. Silenced, after a moment the schnauzer takes a breath and lets it out. He rises on his haunches. —Time for the walk, he says. —Night. The walk, the news, then sleep.

He turns and trots along the brick path at the back of the pool cage. Luger may or may not stop to tell the three Yorkshire terriers about Cliff Gilmore. It depends on whether the Dog speech is still going on in his well-groomed head. Once under way the speeches are hard to stop, something like the prey drive in certain breeds.

—I'm going too.

Rising, Emma now stretches luxuriously. Chiffon also stands. She hates walking alone, and this is also true of her mistress. Like Emma, the bichon was raised from puppyhood by one person. Few would believe how closely such dogs come to resemble their owners.

—What about you?

Bill shakes his head. He is standing again, still intent on the open doorwall. Compared to the other dogs, he is huge.

She turns and begins walking along the brick path. *Buddies.* That's the human word for Bill and Hotspur. Chiffon is not a buddy, but she now catches up and trots alongside.

Vinyl

Bill watches them follow the narrow footpath. From the back they look like littermates, but two dogs could not be more different. Chiffon seems never to have had an actual thought, but Emma has real intelligence. And she knows words, lots of them. Hotspur is smart, too, but border-collie smart. That means something else.

He turns back to the Gilmores' pool cage, hoping the collie will come out. The open doorwall reveals a comfortable interior. Like the house he lives in, it has high ceilings. There are colorful pictures on the walls, furniture and area rugs. Being tall, Bill can see to the front foyer. His long legs and deep chest, his big head and serious face all make him an oddity at Donegal. With few exceptions, the dogs here are small breeds, easily carried on planes or crated in cars.

Again the Gilmore woman appears in the opening. She is tall, with broad shoulders and short red hair. No longer crying, she reaches up and the doorwall rumbles closed. Vertical blinds begin tracking across the glass.

Resigned, Bill flexes long, solid legs, then stretches. Half Labrador retriever, he is black with short hair. His muzzle is longer than those of purebreds, and his height leads people to speculate on his parentage. His broad chest has a white streak, giving him what his missus calls a well-dressed look.

He turns away and regards the jungle rough on the far side of the fairway. Against the deepening night sky it looks thick and black. Maybe the Gilmore missus will feel better when she takes Hotspur for his walk. That's something everyone with a dog has to do. Work, play, death, parties, brunch, church—no matter what, they have to walk the dog. Bill's mister sometimes sees Glenda out with the collie. The next time this happens, he will tell her he is *sorry*.

Bill begins trotting along the brick path in the opposite direction taken by the others. All the houses here have pools and spas protected by screen cages. He passes two with doors and windows already sealed behind hurricane shutters. Come the rain and sultry weather of hurricane season, half the houses at Donegal will look like that.

Sorry. People stopping to talk use the word often at Donegal. Bill's mister always takes off his cap, holding it behind his back as the other person tells about someone who's died or gone to assisted living. Or just had or is about to have surgery. Restaurants, church, scramble tournaments, shotgun starts, owner assessment fees—understanding none of it, Bill waits patiently.

He nears the Telecoms' big house. That's what Madame calls them, Emma's missus. Madame is one of the original residents at Donegal, and she knows telecom stock is how the family made its money. Inside, both white-haired Telecoms are on their red couch, watching TV. They each hold a dachshund, and all four are watching the screen.

Bill continues along the path. The birds have stopped, but insects are diving and buzzing around his head. Although he has floppy ears, they stand high on his head, giving him a vigilant look. It makes some people nervous. Along with being half Labrador, there is German shepherd in him. A quarter of Bill is Great Dane.

Vigilant, yes, but not fierce. Bill is what's called a soft dog. He likes the dachshunds and other small dogs, letting them bounce around and sniff him. Mrs. Telecom loves Mozart, and that explains her dogs' names, Wolfi and Stanzi. Her husband takes them with him when he plays golf. They are a fixture at Donegal, and a source of envy among other dogs. How can you not feel envy, seeing them seated side by side on a platform between golf bags, their small, proud heads raised as the cart trundles over the course? Before hurricane season, they fly north, in a satchel placed under the missus' seat. When they get there, the car is waiting, shipped in a truck.

As he nears the Vinyl house, Bill trots faster. His hearing grows precise, ears more erect. He was saved by his mister, and there is nothing Vinyl can ask that Bill won't do. Reaching the screen cage, he sees the man inside, on a chaise. It fills the dog with longing. The reading lamp is on, Vinyl stretched out next to the pool reading a magazine. A sound comes from Bill's throat, something between a whine and a yodel. It's impossible not to love what he sees, impossible not to want to be with the man—lying, sitting, walking—anywhere at all.

The mister lowers the latest issue of *Time*. "Old Bill, old scout—"

The cage's screened door was designed to open out, but Vinyl has reversed it. Bill places his left paw on the frame, and shoves. Quickly he noses in and begins slipping through. Door and frame rub his sides. Sometimes when he isn't quick his tail gets banged—but not tonight. The door claps shut as he trots over. The mister is sitting up, ready to greet him.

"Good old dog, old Bill, what've you been up to?" Using both hands, he begins scratching the dog's neck. Now he scratches behind the ears. I love it, Bill thinks, eyes closed. Always the same, every time. "You digging anywhere? Don't be digging, Bill, no more of that, right? We agreed, didn't we?"

Digging. Of course not, Bill thinks. Never. Eyes closed, barely able to stand, he feels transported. This perhaps is the best, to be greeted this way and scratched in the best places as the mister speaks to you and you alone.

Vinyl likes it, too. At such times he often thinks about the dog's name. The Depression-era song "Bill" had still been popular in his boyhood, during the war. Fifty years later, having done well in vinyl siding, he sold his business and bought a place in Florida, then one on a lake in Michigan. And two years after that, up in Michigan sometime after eight in the morning, walking as he did every day before breakfast along a tree-canopied dirt road, he had glanced back. Trailing him by fifty feet was a long-legged, skinny stray. "A bag of bones" is how he later put it. For half a mile this went on, until Vinyl at last stopped and waited. Sick with parasites and not yet a year old, the dog was already big. In one of those moments that alter every day to follow, Vinyl put out his hand and the stray touched it with his nose. They had walked home, where Vinyl fed him against the protests of his wife.

The glass slider opens. With the scratching still in progress, Bill looks over as the missus steps out. She dislikes him less now, but that first day she saw him as a nuisance. What if it's sick? she called from the house as they came up the drive. What if it's dangerous? It's a mutt, a mongrel. What are you thinking? No papers, no breeder. We're retired, we don't need the aggravation. Vinyl didn't answer. At the door, he kneeled on the walk and looked in Bill's eyes. He opened his mouth to see the teeth, felt along the ribs, then placed his fingers in the gaps between. He's letting me touch him all over, Vinyl said. He trusts me. They do the choosing, just like women. But the missus had already gone inside. Still kneeling, the man cupped the dog's face. You're a hobo, he said. A Depression dog. Your name is Bill.

"What a nice night," the missus says. "Want some tea?"

"Sounds good."

She is again holding the thing, looking down at it in her arms. For days she's been doing this. Wrapped in cloth, it has a shiny face. The eyes blink as she rocks, and now it makes a sound something like a cat. "What do you think, Bill? This is Jeremy. You'll meet the real Jeremy tomorrow. Yes you will, just as cute as they come."

She reaches down and holds it in front of him. It smells like the shower curtain. He looks up and sees the missus is smiling. She straightens and goes inside. "It's something she read," Vinyl says, still scratching. "She thinks you might be jealous of the baby, so she's getting you ready with a doll. Her middle name is worry."

All Bill understands is that the missus has stopped making a fuss when he's wet. The first time he came out of the lake in Michigan, with the great pleasure of water still delighting the Labrador part of his nature, Bill shook himself on the dock. Mrs. Vinyl yelled about her dress, the chair cushion. She demanded the mister do something—lock the dog in the garage or tool shed—anything, so he wouldn't do what was in his nature, to plunge into the delicious Michigan lake and lunge at fish.

Vinyl stops scratching and sits back. The dog quivers from a strong wish to jump up and sprawl on the man, to mold himself into the presence that loves him, that is warm and generous and walked along the road at the most important time. But he doesn't. Not on the flimsy chaise. On the thing inside, sometimes. It happens when the mister is taken with a need of his own. Usually it happens when the missus isn't with him on the couch. At such moments the small need flows from Vinyl's head and heart to his hand—and he pats the cushion next to him. When this happens, it's like what the missus calls all the things that make her voice happy. Certain people, and things to eat, and weather. She calls them all *heaven*.

But not on the chaise. Bill spreads himself on the cool, smooth concrete at Vinyl's feet. He smells chlorine. Sometimes when it's hot, if the mister is in the pool and makes a certain move—Bill always watches for it, sprawled and panting in the midday heat—if he calls and claps his hands, oh what goodness! It's almost equal to the big lake in Michigan, spreading from sandy shore and dock, out beyond the diving platform.

No. Eyes closed, hearing the phone ringing inside, Bill knows the lake is better than the swimming pool. Better even, he decides, hearing the missus talking now in her high voice, than the times the mister takes him to Naples Pier. Together they walk out over water, filing between rows of men talking, smoking, the air loaded with scents of ocean and fish. Bill feels proud to be taken, sensing eyes on him, hearing questions asked, hands stroking. Then they go down steps to the beach. Yes, that is wonderful, too. *The Gulf*, the mister calls it, tasting of salt. Fish are everywhere, more than at the lake, almost too many. Half asleep now, he remembers barking and lunging, seeing flat, wavy things that flap and scoot, leaving plumes of sand.

Many things make no sense to him. Lying under the dining table is one, looking at the feet of strangers, everyone talking, nicking the plates with knives. Bill stays still and listens, smelling food, smelling strange bodies and shoes and what's on the shoes. Sometimes the voices rise. When this happens, it makes him nervous. Like all dogs, Bill is a pack animal with strong loyalty to his leader. When Vinyl seems for some unknowable reason to not be himself—shouting, banging the arms of his chair—Bill leaves.

The missus comes out again. This time, she doesn't have the doll. "That was Rita Fisk. Cliff Gilmore died two hours ago."

"Oh God."

"He had a coronary playing Frisbee with Hotspur. At the tennis courts. He died in the EMS van."

"Was Glenda with him?"

"Shopping. It was on her answering machine when she came

in. Talk about insensitive. You're shopping, you come in and find out about it that way. Rita's there now. Such a nice man."

"Cliff was a wonderful guy. The best. How's Glenda?"

"Rita says not well. Because she wasn't there. Of course they weren't married all that long, who can really know?"

Vinyl doesn't answer right away. "None of you like her because she's young."

"Don't be silly."

"'Trophy wife, floozy, bimbo—'"

"Rita thought you might be willing to walk Hotspur."

The mister stands and Bill does the same. It is time to walk, and the missus has said *Hotspur*.

"I don't want you hanging out over there."

Vinyl makes the clicking sound he uses to call Bill. "God, the man's dead two hours. Already you think she's husband-hunting." He looks down. "Come on, let's pay Hotsie a visit."

* * * *

It's night, the streetlamps on. They are high up, making their sound. Like small clouds, insects form a shifting mass atop each post. The lights themselves are TV blue.

Bill and Vinyl walk along Donegal Boulevard. The road circles the property and is just over a mile long. Most nights the mister goes toward the clubhouse. Either they walk there and come right back, or Bill waits on the grass, hearing the mister's voice among others in the lounge.

Meeting at such times or on evenings when allowed out, the dogs communicate through gestures and infrasonic noises. They understand some often-repeated sounds—words—but the human world is mostly understood through sense impressions. They pick up on changes in inflection and skin tone, in eye size and electrical discharge. Fear or desire makes itself known through scent and movement. Changes in barometric pressure signal the coming of storms.

When Bill meets other dogs on walks, they are always on leads. He never is, and it makes him proud. From the beginning, Vinyl knew what to do. He had owned dogs before and knew to spend time and be clear. Firm but patient, he trained Bill in a school gym with other dogs and misters. He trained his dog to walk at his side without a leash, to heel, stay, come. Slow or fast, always the dog trots next to his mister's left thigh. When Vinyl stops to speak to someone, Bill sits.

The dogs he sees live in single-family homes. There are other dogs, in townhouses and condos—he hears them across the fairways. But this part of the property is Bill's domain. Sometimes he and Vinyl see Luger, or Chiffon. Sometimes even the Yorkies are walked, a troika on tiny leads, small and busy. There were four, but last winter one fell into his mister's unheated pool. Of the dogs at Donegal, Bill most often sees Hotspur with Cliff Gilmore. The man has a big voice and always makes Vinyl laugh.

They move up a driveway. Bill's flank just touches Vinyl's hip as they step now into the carriage-light glow of the entry. Bill sits. A bell rings, just like the one where he lives. Hotspur barks inside, there are footsteps.

The door opens. "Hello Rita."

"Oh, Fred. Good." Nails are clicking on tile.

"How's she doing?"

"Valium seems to help. Come in."

"Maybe I should just—"

"No no, come in for a minute, it's better if she talks. Hotsie—" She grabs for Hotspur's collar, but the collie slips past. The two dogs begin the greeting ritual at nose and anus.

"It's all right, they'll stay here." The mister goes inside and closes the door. Bill and Hotspur shift from the entry to the front lawn.

—What happened? Bill spreads himself.

—How do I know? Hotspur settles next to him on the grass.
—I'm a dog. It's *Thursday*. That's the day we go to the club. He drinks *beer*, then we go to the *tennis courts* for *Frisbee*. It's like always, nothing different. He throws, I catch, he throws a different direction, I'm there. You know.

Bill knows.

—One minute he's clapping like always, the next he's on his back. Glenda thinks he's dead. Bill looks at the collie. —This happened before, she wasn't there. It's before her. On the Cape. He's *surf-casting*. Does your mister take you to the beach?

—Yes.

—They do it there. *Surf-casting*. Down he goes. The first missus is reading a book. She starts screaming 'What's wrong! What's wrong!' It makes you wonder. 'What's wrong!' She doesn't go for help.

—What happened?

—He's bad, I can tell. I'm up close, looking down at his face. Then I start barking, trying to get the woman to help. She's still yelling 'Cliff, talk to me, what's wrong?' You have to wonder.

—What happened?

—I see she's not doing anything. I run to the neighbors'. A smarter woman, I have to say. What is it, Hotsie, what's wrong? They drive him somewhere. Whatever happens, he comes back. Then the missus dies. This is—I don't know—a long time after Cliff got me. Something was wrong with her. She listened to *polkas*, she called them.

—Why is this one crying if the mister is coming back?

—You see how it is. I knew you were all out there tonight. What can I do? The woman's talking to me. They both do. With Cliff I know everything he means. Everything. This woman is actually better than the first. Don't they do it with you?

Bill nods. All dogs at Donegal have to deal with it. Lectures, jokes, listening mornings to the day's plan while someone sits on the toilet or shaves. —My mister talks when he watches TV, Bill says. —'They're taking him out, what did I tell you? There it is, Bill, the two-minute warning.' I don't understand.

—But you act like you do.

—When he gets going, I don't know what he wants.

—But you stay there.

—What can I do?

—Same with Glenda. They're all different. The first one, always talking to me. Who she's *knitting* for, where they're going on the next *trip*. The second didn't talk at all. I think that's why she left. Glenda talks a lot. When she and Cliff *dance*, when she does *yoga*.

They hear crying inside the house, coming to them on the dark lawn over the buzz of the streetlamp. Hotspur looks to the door, then faces forward. —I can tell this one loves Cliff and me. Sometimes we're alone. He goes in the car or plays golf. She's doing *email* or *cooking*. She looks down, she says, 'Hotsie, we're *lucky* to have him.' You can see from her face and hear it.

Studying the bugs, the shifting, nervous quiver around the streetlamp, Bill understands. Hotspur knows they are lucky to have good misters. Emma understands, too, but in a different way. She is what humans call standoffish.

—Luger thinks crying is wrong, Bill says.

—Because of his mister. Hotspur now stands. —Glenda thinks Cliff is dead. She wasn't there the first time. She thinks the *truck* thing won't bring him back.

The other women at Donegal talk about Glenda Gilmore. In retirement, they are hungry for gossip and think Cliff Gilmore's third wife is a gold digger. They resent the woman, you can hear it in the rise and fall of their voices. Tomorrow, Bill's missus will talk on the phone about her. Others at lunch or over coffee will tell each other to watch their husbands like a hawk whenever Glenda Gilmore is around.

—Are we going to walk? Hotspur is up and pacing now. He

sees something on the far side of the street and tears after it. Bill wants to follow, but stays where he is. When the mister comes out, he has to be here, to show he has learned and remembered.

The collie is trotting back as the front door opens. —Armadillo, he says. —Nothing you can herd.

"OK, boys, let's go."

At last. Reluctantly, Hotspur stops jumping as Vinyl fastens the lead to his collar. However smart they are, however good their training, in the end border collies are all action. Not me, Bill thinks. At the mister's side he walks slowly, proudly. They move toward the street, Hotspur already pulling on the lead.

Madame

The following morning, plantation shutters have been opened in the study. Slats of static brilliance lie on an Oriental carpet, and on all sides bookshelves cover the walls. A Waterford bowl rests on the butler's table, holding a gardenia. The ceiling fan is making its soft luffing sound.

" '—*at last, she was through with lying, cheating and with the numberless desires that had tortured her. She hated no one now; a twilight dimness was settling upon her thoughts, and, of all earthly noises, Emma heard none but the intermittent lamentations of this poor heart, sweet and remote like the echo of a symphony dying away.*' "

The poodle rests next to her mistress on the loveseat. "So foolish," Madame says. She closes the book. "But of course beautifully written. And nicely rendered. This is a new translation by someone named Paul DeMan."

She folds her hands on the jacket and stares straight ahead. "I'm always divided about Emma Bovary. Such a ridiculous romantic. So devoid of self-knowledge. But here, where she makes such a mess of her own death—" Madame shakes her head. "It's impossible not to feel something, don't you think? Because she *is* in pain, isn't she? Not the social discomfort Jane Austen's Emma goes through. She's your namesake, by the way. No, *this* Emma experiences the real thing. Intense suffering, spiritual torment. But how much of it is her own fault, how much is fate?"

Madame is still staring at the wall opposite. She is doing this more now, stopping to think before going on. "By fate, I'm not talking about Zeus and so forth. I'm talking about biology. Genetics."

She places the book on the table. Standing slowly, she moves to the open double doors. Emma steps down from the loveseat and follows, across the foyer to the door leading to the garage. Madame is eighty-four, but neither foolish nor delusional. I'm just old, she tells people. What's all this nonsense about aging gracefully? She opens the door and leans in to push the button. The acrid odor of raw concrete joins the sound of the big garage door rolling up. As this is in progress, she turns and begins moving toward the back of the house. There, bright morning sunlight streams through the expanse of glass that looks out on the lanai. These impressions tell Emma they will be *gardening*. She settles on the smooth wood floor to wait.

When Madame talks—about books, stories in the paper, other people—none of it holds meaning for her dog. But more than any other pet at Donegal, Emma, a chocolate-brown, AKC-registered miniature poodle, knows words. Not like a human, and not just because she's smart—although poodles are clever and high-strung, given to moods. The development of her gift derives from an aspect of her mistress's marriage. Before his death, Archie and "Madame Lydia" Stafford loved reading to each other. Side by side on the sofa or in separate chairs, at the dining table or in bed, one swimming, one stretched out on the lanai, they read novels to each other, the *Times*, articles in *The New Yorker*—sometimes, just for fun, tabloids from the supermarket.

And when Archie died suddenly of a brain aneurism eight years before, his widow had asked her friends about dogs. You know me, she told them. What would be best? But please, no baby substitutes. No lint balls with wet noses. Very well, the friends said. A real dog. Enter a puppy from a new litter of poodles with highly regarded bloodlines.

Even during paper training (Madame called it the Gutenberg phase), Emma's mistress kept her new puppy next to her. As she had done with her son decades before, she traced the words with her finger as she read. Emma listened to the sounds. Not that she learned to read or grasp syntax. But something happened at the end of the second year: Madame read, then reread a book she especially liked. The sounds, the finger tracing lines on the page— I know what this is, Emma thought. This is *reading*.

Now she is coming back, a slow-moving form against brilliant light. "Weeding day, Emma. No rest for the wicked." She has changed into one of the loose cotton dresses worn when doing yard chores. Never shorts. Everyone at Donegal wears shorts all the time. Not Madame. Are we children? she asks. Extras in lederhosen from *The Sound of Music*?

She is very thin and the old sneakers now on her feet make her look more so. Or perhaps it's the hat, a broad-brimmed straw with a green scarf tied to the crown. Emma rises and follows her down the step into the garage. Madame gets her work gloves, bucket and trowel from a shelf in front of the car. "See, Emma? Everything's here, where it belongs."

She shuffles along her ten-year-old gray Mercedes, out the opening to the drive. Already warm, the drive is made of brick pavers. A walkway leads to the front entrance, then around to the back. Emma keeps to Madame's side. Perhaps she will work here, in front. There are two Christmas palms and two pygmy date palms. All are surrounded by impatiens. At the street, bright orange ixora plants form a hedge. Madame stops to inspect one of her date palms. "It's doing well, isn't it? I thought it was dying. All it needed was trimming."

She looks out to the street. The mailbox stands at the end of the drive, but it's too early for mail. Or, she might be thinking to grocery shop, before it turns hot and makes the car an *oven*.

"Was I on the phone?" She looks down at the bucket in her hand, and resumes walking. At the corner, dog and mistress turn. A compressor is rattling behind a trimmed box hedge. As always, Madame says, "That's what keeps the house cool. And that thing there controls the irrigation system."

They move slowly. Madame likes to identify things, instructing her dog as she cooks, holding up the garlic press or spatula, cautioning her sensitive poodle before turning on the noisy microwave or blender. *This cocktail pitcher was one of Archie's favorite things.* She says that every night. The pitcher makes a bell-like sound when Madame stirs her martini.

"And this loud gismo heats the pool. Ken must have called the service. I'm sure I didn't remember. We want them seeing everything is *comme il faut*, don't we? We certainly do, very important. When they get here, we want them to see us hunky-dory."

Ken is the son.

Madame moves slowly now. Emma no longer minds. Some dogs complain they don't get enough exercise. Luger for one. I'm a schnauzer, he says. Mission-oriented, a working breed. Early on she felt the same, even though Madame paid the cleaning lady to exercise her new dog. But in the years since her surgery ("freed from the burden of reproduction," Madame said of it), the poodle feels less edgy and confined.

We're slow together, she thinks as her mistress reaches the unpainted wooden stool. She leaves it out when working in the beds. Sitting carefully, she tucks her dress between her legs and gets the trowel from her bucket. She begins loosening a weed in the mulch under a gardenia bush. They're past their prime, she said yesterday of the flowers. Like me. But heavy-scented blooms still hang among the waxy leaves. And there are hibiscus bushes, and liquala palms at the corners. Not trees, Madame insists. Palms are related to grass. People are always getting that wrong.

Emma settles on the grass, content to feel morning sun on her curly back. "I'm always divided about her—" Madame digs out another weed. "Such a ridiculous romantic. But it's impossible not to feel something, don't you think? She *is* in pain. That's really the question. How much is her, how much is fate—"

She leans forward and drops the stool between the next two bushes. As she sits, a horn sounds. "Hiyee—"

Dog and mistress turn as a golf cart trundles toward them from the middle of the fairway. "You're up early!" the woman calls. It's the Telecoms. Between them, Wolfi and Stanzi sit on their platform looking alert. In dog terms it is annoying, seeing the pleasure the dachshunds take in being the essence of spunky, sharp-nosed privilege. The cart rolls to a stop on the shallow rise leading up to the houses.

"He threw a club."

"I didn't throw it, I dropped it. It broke, plain and simple."

"You don't break a club dropping it. He threw the club, Lydia, don't listen to him. We're on the last hole, the back nine. He shanks it, he takes a big divot on his approach shot. Bingo! into the lake—"

Dressed in coordinated pink-and-green outfits, the Telecoms smile and laugh as they argue. They are full of stories and chatter from the card parties, tournaments and golf banquets that make up their days. It doesn't matter whether others answer or register interest. For them, others serve mostly as silent partners, like pets.

The cart is turning, getting ready to roll back down the fairway. "Tommy Bolt had to teach Arnold Palmer how to throw clubs—" Telecom demonstrates. "Palmer threw them backward, over his shoulder. He got tired walking back to pick them up. Bolt showed him how to throw the clubs in front, like a real professional."

His missus barks a laugh as the cart lumbers off. Turning back,

Emma sees Madame has already resumed her weeding. She smiles as she digs. "Very jovial, weren't they? Renters, I suppose. For some reason, they thought they knew me."

Littermates

Later the same day, lots of activity figures at the Vinyls'. Mornings are mostly quiet, with bran muffins and fruit on the lanai after the walk. Then the newspaper. Tuesdays and Thursdays the mister plays golf, but today no paper, no golf. And the walk was short, only halfway to the clubhouse. When they got back, the missus put her husband to work. He helped change sheets in the front bedrooms, vacuumed furniture. "*You're* the retiree!" he shouted, smiling down as he used the crevice tool.

Bill knows family is coming—the missus keeps talking about *grandchildren*—but he doesn't know who. There is a *son* and a *daughter*. They have both been to the lake, but only the daughter has come here.

No, this time it's the son. Before he comes through the entrance, Bill recognizes the voice, deeper than the mister's. Last summer, he came to the lake with his little boy, *Ronald*. The mister and missus made much of him. There was singing, and lights on something the missus carried in. Then clapping and eating.

This time, following Ronald holding his father's hand comes a woman Bill doesn't know. She is carrying the new pack member. The missus bends and kisses Ronald, then straightens. Looking down, she folds back the cloth and makes the sound from last night. *Jeremy*, she says, over and over.

As this is happening, the girl enters. She, too, came to the lake last summer. Her name is *Ruby*. Older and taller than the boy, she is again staring down at a thing held in both hands. She did this last summer at the lake, pushing buttons, making bell sounds. It's a toy called a *Game Boy*. The mister now stoops and takes her in his arms. The girl smiles, looking over his hug at the hand working the buttons.

The boy pulls free and comes forward. Bill wants to run, but doesn't. He remembers Ronald from last summer. The mister introduced them, moving the boy's hand along Bill's flank—"Nice doggy. See? He won't hurt you. That's it, be gentle. No, not the ears, they don't like that—" Then the mister set the boy on Bill's back—just for a moment, balancing him there, making a joke, the boy laughing.

Does Ron remember? Yes. He is doing it right, running his small hand along the rib cage. At eye level, Bill looks into the boy's face. He is taller, with light-colored hair. Smelling soap and child, he realizes the hair is the same color as Randy, the golden retriever. Randy died. Emma says he lost his hind leg to an alligator.

The boy hugs the dog's neck, but doesn't pull his ears. Good. It's hard to keep still with grandchildren. They are pack members, but do things they shouldn't—touch, pinch, hit. But anything smelling of packchild is *heaven*. Now the boy lets go and runs for the back of the house. "Swimming!" he shouts. "Swimming!"

The missus is still making the sound. Vinyl stands with a sigh. "We're up, Bill. Time to go to work. Come on."

Go to work. Bill trots after. Luger complains of too little work, of the need for a job. You have one, Bill thinks. To do whatever they want, to make them glad you came out of the bushes on the gravel road. Ahead, man and boy turn into the big bedroom. The dog stops before the glass and looks at the pool. They're putting on different shorts. Once in the water, the two will throw balls, and hit each other with long plastic noodles. Or swim to the bottom and come up with coins the mister will let the boy keep.

He turns to look back at the missus. She is holding the new pack member, swinging as she did last night with the doll. He remembers Ruby less well than her brother. At the lake, she went swimming only a few times. She played on the porch with her father, working jigsaw puzzles on the floor. At night after dinner when her brother watched videos, she drew on sheets of colored paper, getting up to show her father, leaning into him each time she gave him a drawing. Or, she made bracelets and necklaces, stringing beads. Bill doesn't remember, but she put one around his neck. She smiled, looking up at her father the way Bill looks at the mister, watching his face, loving his presence.

The new woman is smiling, too, still talking with the missus about the trip. The son has his arm around her, father and mother talking and talking about the new marriage, the new baby. Not smiling, leaning against her father, Ruby keeps working the Game Boy.

* * * *

—We saw it.
—All three of us.
—It happened early. Before the first golfers.
—He ran in front of the thing they use—
—Not the mower, the other thing—

Although they have distinct personalities, the three Yorkshire terriers tend to communicate as one. —The worker almost drove into the sand thing, Lola says in her squeaky dog voice. —Another worker came out. He had something to eat.

—From the grill.

—That's how they grabbed him.
—Luger says the woman made no sense.
—Kept saying *pots*.

The Yorkies live at the Colonel's, in the third house from Madame's. They are telling Emma what happened this morning with Hotspur. The still-grieving Glenda Gilmore let the dog out instead of walking him. He was spotted running on the course. When the greens keeper chased him, Hotspur circled and maneuvered, evading capture. The greens keeper almost tipped over his cart.

—So Luger told you, Emma says.
—Last night. Lola is on her hind legs, paws on the screen.
—He said the man died playing Frisbee.

The three Yorkies stand inside the pool cage. Very tiny (at birth, Yorkshire terriers are weighed with a gram scale), they are both laughable and smart. On the far side of his pool, dressed in shorts and an olive-drab tee shirt with Airborne on the front, the Colonel sits at a glass table. He glances over, then back to the *Naples Daily News*. The dogs are never out of his sight now. Not after what happened last winter to Bama, a male named for the Colonel's favorite football team. Before Bama died in the unheated pool, the dogs were allowed to putter around outside the cage. Not anymore.

—Luger says the wife was nervous-making a long time, Lola says.
—Crying, waving her arms.
—Our missus calls her something.
—Gold digger.
—And tart.
—Running on the course is bad.
—Not done.
—Against the rules.

Madame is calling. Emma turns away and trots along the path. She doesn't know it, but her own mistress never talks behind

Glenda Gilmore's back. Madame doesn't gossip at all, really. When a neighbor comes with stories about this man's drunken singing on karaoke night, or that woman's decision to have a rose tattooed on her ankle (someone in her sixties who should know better), Madame just smiles and nods. But once the neighbor is gone, she looks down at Emma and says, "Someone ought to send her to obedience class, don't you think?"

As she nears the house, a pair of white golf carts trundle by. Lush and moist with the arrival of rainy season, the vivid grass seems to consciously mark the carts' progress with a darker shade of green. The smell of living things, the fresh morning air not yet replaced by midday heat fill Emma with a sense of well-being. She reaches the house and glances again at the fairway. The swampy rough on the far side looks like real jungle. In winter it turns brown, but is now full of water. It serves to irrigate the golf course. Channels and pipes link it to other reservoirs, and sometimes alligators make their way onto the property. Outside the precinct of Madame's comfortable home, it is best to be wary. When Randy lost his leg, a worker claimed a gator did it. Men came and took it away.

As she almost always remembers to do, her mistress has used the wooden gardening stool to prop open the cage's screen door. Emma is big for a toy poodle, but she hops delicately over it. Voices come from inside. *Ken*, and the daughter-in-law. Madame loves visits from her son, but it is better when he comes alone. Before her stroke, she also went to the son's house, arranging twice a year for her cleaning lady to see to Emma. Once back home, she always vowed not to go again. Such a sweet boy, she'd say, dropping into her favorite chair and pulling off her shoes. I hate seeing him led around like a pony. One positive side to growing old, she'd say, looking down at Emma and kneading her bunion, is being able to leave without explaining yourself.

The doorwall is open and Emma enters. They are all seated in the big living room, voices echoing under the vaulted ceiling. Large, gilt-framed pictures hang on the walls. They come from a house in Chicago Emma never saw. Standing in the room's corners are tall Chinese urns filled with brightly colored silk flowers.

She stands a moment and studies the daughter-in-law. The woman is staring down at the floor. On every visit she does this, clucking her tongue, pointing and speaking with too much animation. Madame believes that when she dies, the first thing her daughter-in-law will do after the funeral is call a contractor and have the floor planks shipped to her own house in Palm Beach. They are real Florida cypress, taken up in a house scheduled for demolition and sold at auction. This is *not* gossip, Madame said, still kneading her bunion. This is simple deduction. She wants this floor.

"Emma! Hello there!"

"Hi, Emma." Ken is seated next to his mother on one of the couches, his wife opposite in a wingback chair.

"Well, now, I think we may have put on a pound or two there, old girl. Am I right, Lydia?"

"Do you think so? I hadn't noticed. I do spoil her."

"But so cute. Look at that face, it's like she understands every word."

"I think we'd all be surprised to know just how much they understand. And some of us would be very embarrassed."

The daughter-in-law's laugh bounces around the vaulted ceiling. None of them hear it, but Emma detects a tinkling in the crystal chandelier in the dining room. She doesn't really want to, but Ken is a pack member, so she now steps to the couch and stands before him. He reaches down and scratches the top of her head. It's not where she wants scratching, but she stays to be polite.

"We want to take you to dinner," the daughter-in-law says. "You always go to so much trouble when we visit. It isn't right."

"Don't be silly, I like doing it. Emma and I are grateful when you come."

"Oh, I know, and it's always terrific, but you put yourself out so. It's embarrassing."

"Nonsense. I have everything planned."

"Are you eating at the club these days, or alone here?"

"I'm afraid the club menu isn't much just now. We like it here, don't we?"

Knowing she is being spoken to, Emma closes her eyes as the son scratches.

"Isn't it lonely? Don't you want company?"

"We worry, Mom. We're over there on the other side of the state, wondering how you're doing. In this big house all alone. Cooking, driving in all this traffic."

"Have there been any more tickets? We really do worry, you know."

"The traffic's much better now. When the snowbirds leave, it's like the old days around here."

Madame almost never lies, but there *have* been more tickets. Two. One for turning from the wrong lane on Fifth Avenue, one for running a red light on Third. Emma was in the car both times, the officer leaning in, tipping his hat and asking to see the license. Not knowing who he was, Emma barked. Then Madame drove away, the stiff yellow card on her lap.

"I think I'll freshen up." The daughter-in-law stands.

The son stops scratching and stands as well. "Me too. You'd think I'd driven all the way from Tallahassee or Pensacola, I'm that tired."

"We're all getting older, aren't we?" The daughter-in-law stretches her arms and smiles. "I just can't get over this floor."

The Bad Thing

"Go on! Get it! Do it!"

Ronald stands with feet poised, his back to the cage. Dripping and glossy, Bill prances and dodges before him, watching the ball. The boy makes as if to throw, and again. Each time, the dog stays where he is. He understands now to hold out for the actual toss, the real one. And he has learned that if he waits but then finally barks, the boy throws. So now he barks, eyes locked—and the boy throws.

The dog spins and takes off over the deck. At pool's edge he launches himself, fully extended, landing as Labs should land with his head above water and legs already in motion. The mister is at the deep end clapping, cheering him on. It is the best thing about children coming, the mister playing this way. Bill reaches the ball, takes it, turns, and begins swimming for the shallow end. There are stairs, the way out. Retrieving is just half the mission, he has to get the ball back, return and drop it at the boy's feet. That way, the game will go on as long as the boy has interest, something Bill never lacks.

Again, and again. The boy switches to the big ball, the one used with the net at the deep end. It's too big to grab, but Bill noses and shoves it in front of him, trying to grab it, failing, trying, the thing bobbing. Sometimes he gets a paw on it, then it pops away—but he goes on trying.

The boy's father likes shooting baskets, but has gone in to be with his new wife and the baby. Now there are just the three of them. Bill does not know where the girl is. "OK, grandpa's got something he has to do." The mister is working his way to the ladder.

"Aw, not yet, come on, just another—"

"When I get back from the funeral home. Then it's you, me and Bill, OK? That's a promise."

So, it's over. Bill understands less than Emma does of what is said by humans. He lived only with dogs his first year, in a kennel. A puppy mill it was called. The litters were quickly weaned, the mothers mated over and over until used up, then destroyed. He and his littermates had been a mistake, the result of a Lab bitch and a Great Dane mix left unattended by the breeder's cousin.

But Bill's instincts are excellent, and he knew the play would be over soon. He reaches the stairs and splashes up. Paws firmly planted, he shakes himself, and again. The boy is slapping his wet back, and now the mister comes with the towel. *Bill's towel* he calls it, always used before he is let inside.

The boy runs through the open doorwall as the mister rubs. "How was that? Was that good? You bet it was. Old Bill, good dog. That boy's nuts about you."

He understands only *good*, his name, *boy*. But he knows the voice, its many ups and downs, loud or soft. Knows the smells of anger and fatigue, eyes that make him look away, or say to stay right here with me. They look that way now. The mister stops with the towel and cups Bill's muzzle in his hands. Vinyl doesn't much like it, but sometimes at such moments Bill has to lick his face. He chances it now, because water is his medium and it makes him think at such moments—it *is* a thought—how good it is to have been dying in the woods but to make a choice, to come out of scrub undergrowth and follow this man into all that has come since.

"Attaboy. You hold down the fort. We'll take the kids for a walk later." Vinyl stands and Bill walks at his side, into the cool house.

* * * *

They are going somewhere, just the missus and mister. They are in the bedroom putting on different clothes. The missus smells like flowers, talking before the mirror. The mister, too, smells the way he does in the morning, like lemons.

They are done. He follows them from the bedroom, glancing back through the house to the deck. The pool lies motionless. In the last half hour, the water has changed color, and this troubles him. He turns away and follows the couple to the garage entrance. The mister looks down. "Not this time. Sit." Bill sits. "You hold down the fort, back in an hour."

They go down the step and the door closes. From the other side comes the rumble of the garage door. He looks back through the dark house as the car backs out. Again comes the rolling sound, then nothing. He walks slowly toward the glass doorwall, past furniture he mustn't scratch, couches not to be jumped on.

He stops before the glass. The bigger ball floats, and the long things they hit each other with. But the water is gray-green, the grass beyond so dark. He whines. It rains almost every day now. Not like rain at the lake. Even alone in the woods, having escaped the kennel and sick from parasites, Bill had not been afraid. There, rain was just a pattering through trees. The ground beneath stayed dry.

But here. When it rains here, everything disappears beyond the pool cage—the golf course, the jungle rough. Even so, that isn't what now causes him to whine and raise his paws, to salivate looking out. Not now, Bill thinks. Not now. It's bad when the mister is here, but without him—

A seam, a sharp-edged broken white line blinks and is gone. He spins and runs back through the house, seeing the girl a second with the toy in her hand before he scuttles, hindquarters low, back into the mister's bedroom. He flattens himself and pulls with his front paws, still working his bulk under the bed when it comes. Whining, he keeps working as thunder batters—falling, dropping like the big barrels for trash but much worse, terrible. Fully under the bed, he feels no safer. He feels safer when the mister is here, saying something in his calm voice, saying it's all right, hold on, Bill, it'll be over soon, just a squall, nothing to worry about, hang in there.

What do they know? Nothing of the man who shot bottles behind the kennel, his rifle making just that sound. Or the one who cut logs with something angry and loud—the same one who put weaker pups or mistakes in a sack and carried them to the lake. Except when he was curious. That's why Bill was spared, a mistake, yes, but big—who could say how big? Not all Lab, but maybe a good retriever, a dog for home use instead of sale. Keep him and see.

The noise of rolling thunder stuns him. Somewhere the baby is crying. Bill tries to flatten even more, knowing he has done a bad thing. Nowhere to go, nothing to stop the sound. Once more it moves the whole house, rattles windows and again he feels himself doing the bad thing. Just because the mister always comes back, how can you say he will this time? Thinking that is worse than the woods had been, cold and gray. Chased from garbage cans and dumpsters, boys throwing rocks, handsful of gravel. No, this is worse. The *noise* of it, but mostly the not knowing—

"Where are you?"

The wrong voice. Not the mister or missus. The girl. But any voice at all gives relief, and Bill whines in answer. The thing they keep on the bed is raised. She is lying on her side, on the floor, looking at him. Still she holds it up. "Are you scared?" He wishes she would leave, let go of the cloth and leave him in darkness, not stare at him. But she goes on looking at him, saying nothing.

Then the girl does something even the mister never has. With the noise going on—so loud he can't help the bad thing each time it comes—she now covers herself with the bedspread—and stays there. On her side next to the bed, she lays her head on the carpet facing him. She says nothing, no quiet words in the soft voice of the mister when it's like this. Even the missus knows how awful it is for him, getting down and raising the bedspread, saying poor guy, I don't like it either. But then she drops the cover and leaves.

Not the girl. She stays. And as the baby cries somewhere, still Ruby studies him. This has never happened. For a moment he almost forgets the thunder. It's something in her face. Like the Gilmore woman last night. Twice Glenda came outside, crying but silent, circling the pool. Hotspur was at her side. The woman's eyes were like those in front of him now. Under the bed it's dark, but he can see Ruby looking at him.

Border Patrol

"Frankly, I don't see any point in walking him now."

"Honey, it's just a little pee. It's because we left him alone."

"He wasn't alone. There were four people here. Five with the baby."

"Honey—"

"Oh fine, go on, you always do what you want anyway. Go walk your dog."

When she is like this, the missus always says *your* dog. But hearing *walk*, Bill is very happy. After the thunder stopped, the girl dropped the bedspread and left. Bill stayed where he was until the garage door rumbled. They came back, he thought. They're here. He pulled and twisted his body free and ran to the entrance. When they came in he scolded them—where *were* you! why *went* you!— it was his right and the mister knew it. But then the missus found the bad thing, leading from the doorwall and trailing in spots to the bedroom.

She made the mister move the bed. Saying nothing, they changed clothes in the separate little rooms where they each keep things. Now, as Bill and the mister look in, the missus is on the floor, working on the rug.

"We'll do Hotspur. Back in less than an hour."

She says nothing. On the way out, the mister stops outside the TV room. "Anyone want to come for a walk?"

Ruby shakes her head. She is on the couch working the toy. Bill remembers her on the floor with him, her eyes like Glenda Gilmore's. Her brother is seated before the set and doesn't move. The girl looks over. "Is he in trouble?"

"A little bit. Grandma likes things nice."

"So does my dad. That's why he got divorced."

Her grandfather waves and they leave. He closes the heavy front door. "It's rough." They move down the drive. "Her mother calls twice a week, isn't that nice? I don't know. I try to stay out of it. I just feel sorry for Ruby and Ron."

He doesn't understand, but the mister has spoken softly. He has other soft voices—for praise or fatigue or talking to himself. This tone he uses when speaking just to Bill. Overhead float a few big, puffy thunderheads. All of them are white, the air still smelling of rain and lightning-charged ozone. Water has gathered in small depressions on either side of the street. Bill doesn't care, it's good again. The storm has passed, the mister is back. Bill moves next to him with pride, having forgiven.

Golfers have resumed play. It's late afternoon. Birds once more sound in the tall pines between houses. A plane drones, a police siren. Now comes the funny *clink* of someone teeing off. Instinct sets the dog's muscles, but he knows better and relaxes. His first walk here, Bill chased one of the balls. Forgetting everything from the nights in the gym with other dogs, on hearing the *clink* and seeing something flying, he took off. Hearing Vinyl's shouts but riveted on the white thing bouncing down the inviting sweep of grass, he raced after, retrieved it, brought it back and dropped it at the mister's feet. People in the carts laughed as Vinyl returned it. After that, he began taking the dog to the course early, before the golfers, on a lead. The mister said "Stay!" each time before hitting. It was hard, Bill kept running. You couldn't just watch a ball fly, you had to go. But each time, the long lead jerked him back, Vinyl standing on it as he hit. They had done this until the dog understood. It was hard, but he mustn't run, because he wanted to be the best dog, the one the mister had stopped for and fed.

They reach the end of the street and turn onto Donegal Boulevard. Across the median, three women and two carts are stopped on the fairway. A fourth woman is off from the others, looking down, searching. Humans do this a lot, even when the white balls are right there to smell and see.

The Gilmore house faces Donegal Boulevard. Reaching the drive, Bill hears Hotspur inside. There are many barks, some to gain attention, others to express anger, still others to signal a wish to play. As they walk up the drive, Bill hears a bark of fear and confusion. Border collies bark very little, using eye contact to intimidate whatever they herd. Now, as dog and master step under the entrance canopy, something wrong is happening—the collie is clawing the front door, scratching, calling.

"Okay, buddy, that's okay, just a second—"

The mister has a key. "Hold it hold it—" The collie's nose is jammed in the crack, the dog still barking as Vinyl grabs for the collar. "Yes yes—" He has it and shoves in. Bill waits, follows. The mister moves in, holding the collar until he can shut the door. He lets Hotspur go but still the dog barks.

"Jesus—"

He walks into the house, Bill behind. It's the same as his own—bedrooms and TV room in front, the vaulted central hall leading back to the big room. As the freed collie jumps and barks, Vinyl stops. "What a mess." Pillows have been torn apart, a dining chair lies on its side. Next to it rests a wooden salad bowl. There are napkins and napkin rings, a shredded newspaper, the smell of blood.

"The storm." Vinyl begins picking things up. "You guys really hate hurricane season." He carries the torn paper and pillows into the kitchen, then comes back. "We'll call Glenda and give her a heads-up on this. You're not helping matters much, Hotsie."

—I peed, Bill says as Hotspur passes him. —They left me during the storm.

—The storm is bad, that's not it. Hotspur passes again, circling furniture. —What can I do? She's crazy, she's making *me* crazy. She thinks he died, she keeps going on about not being there. Yesterday? You think that's all of it? Hotsie passes again. —He's out there, I know it. He's not dead, nothing's wrong. He has no car. He's waiting for her, what's she doing? She's here on the phone talking and talking. Her mind's gone. I don't know why. All I know, Glenda is making a mistake and I'm going crazy. Cliff and I have our schedule, he knows me, we *do* things —

The collie stops before the glass, looking out at the pool and fairway. The glass is smeared with blood and saliva. The dog whines, turns and again circles. —I'm this certain kind of dog, he knows it. We go to the beach, we do the Frisbee, all the time, every day we're doing something, jobs, we have a schedule—

"Okay, guys, let's go."

The mister is back with the lead. When Hotsie circles in front of him, he grabs him and clips it on. "No, you don't like it, but that's the way it's got to be—" As Hotspur pulls toward the front of the house, the mister's arm jerks. He looks down. "And you behave yourself, hear me?"

He does. Walking next to the mister, Bill is anxious to make up for the bad thing earlier, knowing to listen, obey, to be the best dog. Especially now, with Hotsie straining, coughing.

"Jesus, look at this door—"

They are out now, heading down the walk. Still Hotsie pulls. "I don't know, buster. You better hope Glenda can pick up the drill. Maybe some Valium might help you too—"

—See? Hotsie lets up some, looking back a second at Bill, trying to relax and walk, not pull. —I like her, he says in Dog. That's what's wrong. She comes to the beach, at night she throws tennis balls, they both do. After dark we do it on the course, against the rules but we do it. After they drink wine, letting me know to be quiet, which I am, why would I ruin a thing like that? See? Breaking rules to give me some work. I don't know—

Watching the collie walking now, more or less the right way but staring ahead at nothing—not at something he's herding and locked on, but at nothing—it's confusing.

—She lies on the bed. With the box of paper. For hours. She doesn't know he's waiting for us. I'm going crazy and she just lies on the bed.

—Do you bring the lead? You have to sometimes, for them to know it's time.

—The lead, the Frisbee. Tennis balls, golf balls. I'm up on the bed looking down at her, giving her my stare. She lifts the arm off her eyes, she says, 'I'm so sorry, Hotsie, but I just can't.' Like that.

—Maybe your mister is gone.

Hotspur sees something out on the course. So fast, Bill thinks as the collie, somehow knowing in the instant what to do jumps, seizes the lead in his teeth and snatches it from Vinyl's hand.

"Dammit—"

He's gone, across the street to the median, leaping there to clear plants. Bill is gone now too, the mister yelling as his dog's big body barrels forward but swerves, Bill knowing as he nears that the plants are too tall, tall himself but no jumper, no Hotspur. Dodging left, he finds where a croton has died. Out the other side, he sees the collie has already reached the golfers. Barking on the fairway, circling the women, the dog lunges one way, then the next. The women make sounds and run to the carts. As they do, the dog spins and races toward the lone woman still looking for her ball. Bill lopes across the course as she straightens and sees Hotspur coming. He veers, racing at her. She screams, running now clumsily toward the carts, an old-lady run. The collie circles her, barking, nipping— back and forth, pure herding instinct and method.

Bill comes to a stop. He watches as the three other women huddle behind the cart, afraid. The running woman reaches them, crying, Hotspur barking, keeping them there.

—Smell it?

—What?

—In there. The thing that got Randy—

Bill looks out at the hanging grey-green mass of foliage. Many smells reach him from the jungle rough. Rot, dead and live birds, snakes, the scent of possum and raccoon, squirrels.

—I don't smell it.

—It's there, Hotspur barks in Dog. The mister is shouting, trotting from the road. —I have to keep her from going in. Because of the thing that got Randy. For good measure, the collie begins circling the carts. It works—the women stumble aboard. They are all talking at once, Vinyl calling "It's all right! Don't be afraid!" He chases the lead, stepping and missing, missing again.

If Bill were as smart as Emma, he might later mark what's happened today—the storm, doing the bad thing under the bed, chasing after Hotspur—as the starting point. Who can say which moments of smallest consequence nevertheless shape and direct the future?

But he isn't Emma, or Hotspur. He knows only that the mister is mad at both dogs. *Why* is not the issue. Finally Vinyl manages to step on the collie's lead, apologizing to the women as he drags the dog back to the road. "And *you're* in deep doo doo," he says to Bill, frowning. The dog looks away, ashamed, once more where he belongs, trotting at the mister's side. A mistake, he thinks. Please, no leash, it won't happen again. If he walks straighter than ever, slows perfectly and sits even before the command at each corner, maybe the mister will see his dog is *sorry*.

Hotspur?

Mission accomplished, he is walking now like old times, just as he always does with Cliff Gilmore. The collie has a spring in his step, eyes alert. Vinyl now has the lead wrapped around his wrist. "No more funny business," he says.

The collie keeps walking, eyes straight ahead. —I suppose there's no chance of Frisbee, he says. —No beach.

—The only time my mister throws the Frisbee is in the pool, Bill says.

—He thinks I just felt like scaring the women?

—I don't know. Emma knows a word for what you're doing.

—What's that?

—You change when your mister is gone. You do things you shouldn't.

—You didn't smell the thing? That woman was wandering around next to their swamp. You can't see them unless they move. They look like logs. Cliff sees them on the course, he showed me one. That's what got Randy.

They walk on in silence, feeling the pavement warm under their pads. Some smells here are the same as smells in Michigan, some different. More tall pines rise on the right. Through them can be seen a white scoop of sand, like the beach. Beyond the sand trap stretches another broad fairway. It flows into the distance and looks misty. There are houses on both sides, and the aroma of grilled meat. Dark pine needles carpet the ground under the trees. On walks when coming to this point, Bill often thinks of the Michigan lake, and the woods. He slept on pine needles just like these, curled and hearing wind high up. He was sick, too sick to chase food. He ate grass and threw it up.

—Cliff knows me, Hotspur says. —We're a team.

The collie is still walking in his regular, head-low, high-stepping way, but the stare at nothing is back.

—I'm thinking and thinking, he says. —All day. He's not at the clinic, he'd come back by now. He's at the beach. Glenda still thinks he's dead. Someone took him to Naples Pier and left, he has no car. All this time he's waiting, wondering where I am.

* * * *

An hour later, Emma, lying next to her mistress, is listening to half a conversation about what happened.

Madame is taking the call in her room, propped on the bed and being polite. "Well, it would scare you, wouldn't it? Unless you know Hotspur, how could you be sure?" Seeing her own dog looking at her, she winks. "Yes, he's a very nice man. He was walking them both, so I'm sure he felt responsible—"

She makes the talky-talky sign with her hand. Emma slips off the bed and walks into the front room. She sees the day has deepened almost to evening. If she asked to be let out—gave the signal—Madame would oblige. But she doubts others are out tonight. The ground will still be soggy, and owners don't like dogs coming in wet. She turns away and moves through the house. No meal is cooking. That means they are going out. It's why Madame is resting up. She said the son was a *pony*, whatever that is. Just now, he's in the study, typing on his computer.

The wife is sitting in the TV room, off the front entrance. That's where Madame drinks her evening martini, where she watches the news or *Masterpiece Theatre*. Most evenings she falls asleep, waking when Emma noses her hand. The poodle thinks TV serves her mistress in the way the clock she put in her new puppy's box had served. As a source of company, like a heartbeat.

But the daughter-in-law isn't watching TV. Dressed for going out and strongly scented, she is reading. Next to her are papers like the one in her hand. Not a book, something with pictures.

It would be hard to explain why or how the daughter-in-law knows that Emma neither likes nor trusts her. The poodle has never bared her teeth or barked at the woman—but she does know. She senses the dog's presence and looks over. "You're going to be a problem. If you were a toy, that would be different. And you're long in the tooth, too. I don't see any way around it."

The woman puts down the brochure and stands. She smooths her dress and moves into the hall. "Where are you?"

"In here."

Heels hard on the cypress floor, she walks to the study. They are talking. After a moment, the dog steps into the TV room. She jumps up on the couch to see what's there. Pictures. People are playing cards or eating at tables. Others are swimming in a pool, still others getting on a bus, waving. Another shows a woman in a sunny room seated before a window sill crowded with dolls. On her lap rests a cat.

Real? Unreal? It's hard to know. But in the photo opposite, a man sits on a swing, like the ones outside the Donegal clubhouse entrance. At his side and looking up at him is a breed of dog Emma doesn't recognize. It's small, something like the Yorkies, but different.

She can't know that the brochures concern assisted-living, something Madame often talks about. "A little memory trouble," she'll say, digging weeds. "So now it starts. Oh, they won't work a hard sell, Emma. Nothing pushy. Not at first, anyway. They'll just insinuate the notion. The plausible, logical idea. Which it is. The size of my house, all the service people involved. What happens in hurricane season if the air conditioning goes out. 'All this lightning, mother, it's no joke, we worry.'" Madame smiles, smoothing out the mulch under a gardenia bush. "What do you bet they've set up some visits?"

But if Emma doesn't know any of this, she does know she dislikes the daughter-in-law. She hops down and steps into the hall. Passing the study, the poodle glances in and stops. The son and his wife are sitting side by side on Madame's loveseat. Seeing this tweaks the dog with a small, proprietary sense of violated territory.

"Just the two?"

"Just two."

"I wasn't sure they'd tell you."

"I explained. I gave them my license if they wanted to confirm I was the son."

"I'm surprised there aren't more."

"It's not so bad, is it? Hell, two tickets in two weeks. That could just be bad luck. That could be you or me."

The daughter-in-law sighs. She picks up the crystal bowl with the gardenia and holds it to her nose. She puts it back. "You still think it's wrong."

"I want her to have things the way she wants them for as long as possible."

"Sweetheart, who wouldn't? Do you want her to break a hip? End up in a body cast? People don't last that way, it breaks their spirit. I'm not the enemy here. It's hard, but sometimes the hard thing's the best thing."

She reaches again and picks up *Madame Bovary*. It's lying face down, open to the page Madame likes best. As the daughter-in-law reads, Ken picks up the rose bowl and holds it to his nose.

"Wasn't this here last time?" She holds it out for him to see. He puts down the bowl and takes the book. He reads and doesn't answer.

"I remember hearing her reading to herself. That very passage. I'm telling you, sweetheart, it isn't going away. Think about it. *That* passage, over and over. Who knows how many times? This is not rocket science."

Emma moves to the back of the house. In her room, Madame is no longer on the bed. She is in her walk-in, getting ready to be taken to the restaurant. She looks over. "Hello there. Where have you been? Someone called." She is moving things on hangers. "It was about Hotspur, the Gilmores' dog." She turns to the second row and begins scraping hangers. "Something about chasing people."

Family Romance

Come the hot-weather months, dogs at Donegal eat much less. The same is true of their owners: less golf and tennis mean smaller meals. And shorter walks, fewer trips to the park.

Not Bill. Because of the visiting grandchildren, he is eating even more than usual. When mealtime comes, he's there and waiting in the kitchen, looking up and already salivating as the mister mixes everything—dry food with warm water and chicken broth. Any delay—a phone call, the missus calling the mister to come see something on TV—makes Bill whine and pace. The smell makes him drool, especially when something is being added up on the counter from the mister's own food of the day before. *Steak*, half a leftover *pork chop*. He certainly knows what *fish* means. Twice he caught one in Michigan, wading out and against all odds plunging his big head just right into the cold, spring-fed lake.

Vinyl always feeds him. It's something the missus insisted on as a condition of keeping Bill. When he at last bends down with the weighted bowl, hardly has it touched the floor before Bill is snatching and gulping. In part this is simple instinct, but also memory of starving in the woods. Once, Ronald came into the kitchen to watch. When he approached, without knowing Bill made a sound.

"No, Ron," the mister said. "Stay away when he's eating. Dogs are different."

The boy had gone out and come back with Ruby. "Look," he said.

"Gross. He doesn't even chew."

"Their stomachs are different," the mister explained.

Every day they are in the pool. The boy never tires of faking the throw, making the big dog take his running leap. Or, Ronald braces himself on the deck and pulls at the rope toy until he either lets go or is pulled head first into the pool. That's how strong Bill is. But careful. He understands what they are, that they are small and that he is expected to remember this. Also on walks. The first few times Vinyl went out with the children, he taught Ruby the Sit, Stay and Come commands. Bill soon understood he was to listen to her and obey as he did the mister. But not the boy, he's too small.

Against the missus' protests ("What about the other day with Hotspur?"), Vinyl and his son have agreed to allow Ruby to walk Bill alone. The dog understands perfectly what this requires, what the mission demands. When they reach the fenced place near the big road leading to town, Ronald throws the tennis ball. Bill retrieves, trailing the lead. To be on the safe side, Vinyl has put it on. This happened last summer, at the lake. The lead wasn't necessary, but Bill understood. It has to do with Ruby's being a *grandchild*.

Even so, the girl never goes anywhere without the Game Boy. Inside or out, leaving to go in the car or ride the golf cart, she has it. But something's wrong. He knows their names, and hears them spoken often when Vinyl and the missus talk softly in their room. This is mostly at night, Bill on the floor at the foot of the big bed.

"She seemed happier last summer."

"She had her daddy all to herself."

"You can't blame the stepmother. Ronald seems fine."

"Blame is not the issue, honey. Ruby and her dad have always been kindred spirits. By the time she was five, she was really the wife. She ate with him, they went to movies. Her mother was never home, remember? It started falling apart right after Ron was born."

"And now another baby."

"Exactly. It's not just the new mom, it's the little rival."

He doesn't understand, of course. Only the names register as he lies on the rug, ears shifting with each noise in the house—compressors, ice makers, a plane taking off at Naples airport two miles away that no one else in the house can hear.

Or, he dreams. He never remembers, but wakes several times a night, aware of having treed a squirrel, of leaping at or cornering something with small eyes. Then he gets up and wanders the dark house. Plug-in night lights glow here and there on the floor. They are new and must have to do with the visiting pack members.

At night, the two other big humans take the baby and close their door. But the room where the girl and boy sleep is open.

When Bill looks in, sometimes the girl is still awake, on her back with the bedside light on, the Game Boy held above her head. She has light brown hair that looks red in sunlight. Her skin is pale, the result of her stepmother insisting she and her brother use lots of sunscreen. Her eyes are blue, and if he knew the word, Bill would say they are soulful. Now, each time she looks at him he remembers the eyes from the storm. She has big hands and feet. Their grandmother says they have grown ahead of schedule and are waiting for the rest of Ruby to catch up. Just like her father, the mister says. Exactly the same at her age, remember? Two peas in a pod.

* * * *

It's the first of June, near the end of the visit. The mister and missus have already started gathering things for their own trip north. Bill knows this from the way Vinyl is packing boxes, getting the crate down from the attic in the garage. When it's finally time, he'll put the crate in the van, swing open the door and clap his hands. Once Bill is inside, Vinyl will turn the crate, so the dog can see him and the missus. If he could, Bill would explain the crate isn't needed any more than the lead. He loves the road, especially on short trips to town. He loves it most when allowed to sit in the seat next to Vinyl, head out the window. It's almost too much, the rush of odors, the flood of air. But crate or not, Bill will soon be happily sprawled, numb and sleepy from road vibration.

In the morning, Vinyl rises early, walks and feeds Bill. He makes breakfast for his son, then they go out to the garage. The door rumbles. They get in the golf cart and leave. The new wife and the missus get up later. After breakfast with the children, they go next door with the baby. Ruby is to watch her brother. Often when alone, the two children fight. With pillows, the pool noodles, over toys and puzzles. At first, it bothered him. He barked and whined, wanting them to stop. This was before he was scolded, before he understood it was play of some kind.

But this morning, Ruby refuses to fight *or* play. Learning her father has already left, she sits at the kitchen table in an oversized tee shirt, shoving her toaster waffle around on the plate. Once the two are alone, Ronald works a magnet toy as his sister pushes buttons and frowns. Soon tired of the magnets, he asks her to help him do a jigsaw puzzle. Do it yourself, she says. When he begs her to work the DVD player so he can watch *Toy Story*, she ignores him.

He pulls open the doorwall, goes out on the lanai and looks at the pool. Both he and his sister are forbidden to go in unsupervised. He knows from painful experience this order is not to be ignored. Denied and thwarted, he goes inside and puts on his sandals—his grandmother has warned about fire ants. Once more on the deck, he opens the reversed screen door and steps outside the cage. In the days since his family's arrival, many more residents have left for cooler weather. The morning is silent, the fairway below verdant and peaceful. Not for the first time he wonders about the stretch of undeveloped property on the far side. Birds there are singing, a hawk floating overhead.

Bill has followed him onto the deck, watching as the door's pneumatic closer sighs. Aware of heat on his back, he watches Ronald outside the screen cage, walking. The boy reaches the brick path and moves down the slope leading to the fairway. Ronald looks to the right, shading his eyes, walking. Still moving, looking now to the left, he drops his hand. No father, or grandfather. Into this moment devoid of distractions, he reaches the fairway. Curiosity returns about the trees and dense undergrowth opposite. Back home in Pennsylvania, vacant lots in the subdivision where he lives hold many possibilities. Frogs, butterflies, chipmunks.

As Bill watches, women are laughing and talking in the house next door. He turns and trots inside, back to the girl's bedroom. On her back with the toy, Ruby looks over. After a moment, she says, "You have long legs, too." With her back flat on the bed, dressed in shorts and polo shirt, she looks at the ceiling. She puts the toy on her chest and places her hands flat at her sides. She raises her legs. They are freckled and smooth. She holds them there, wiggling her toes. "Dad says I'm going to be a long drink of water. Mom's tall too. She called last night. She quit smoking again. I asked her why she started in the first place. Dad says he smoked in college, but not since. He comes to my soccer matches back home. When he can."

Agitated, the dog comes to the bed. The girl's eyes rest on him. She seems to be waiting for something, an act or sound. "You want to play ball." Ruby touches his head. "Maybe later." She lowers her legs and takes up the toy.

Bill turns away and trots once more through the house. Outside the cage, on the sunny sweep of turf below, the boy is nearing the jungle rough. The dog barks and the boy turns. The dog barks again, but the boy faces away and resumes walking. Whining, circling the pool, looking out and remembering the women golfers, Bill goes to the door. He paws the frame. This works only from outside. He pushes and rattles the thin door, whining, looking out at the moving boy. The pack-leader collie smelled something, Hotspur knows things, he herded the women. Grandchildren are *heaven*, they walk Bill, the boy pets him the right way, no longer pulls his tail as he did at the lake. He belongs to the mister, Bill senses. Like you—

Thick-nailed and big-shouldered after eighteen months of food and care, the dog claws the screen. It flexes, gives—a tear forms. He shoves head and shoulders through. Laughter comes again from next door as he pushes himself through, clearing his hindquarters. Dashing now, taking divots, the mister would call them, Bill runs to the slope and down, barking, remembering Hotspur and racing over freshly mowed lawn.

Hearing the pummeling on his grandparents' lanai, Ronald has turned to see. Although six and big for his age, he has no pet of his own. There are dogs in cartoons, there's Clifford, and *Lady and the Tramp*. A friend has an English sheep dog, a big, floppy mop that mostly sleeps. Those are the dogs he knows. But Bill is coming so fast, much faster than the boy has seen him move, barking, with big teeth in a mouth that snatches food and once made a sound when Ronald got near—

That's all the boy knows. Bill reaches and passes him. He turns and goes on barking, jumping, grass clippings flying off big paws. The boy screams. It's having seen him eat, having heard the sound, and the dog's size, the way he can jerk Ron into the swimming pool. And because now, whenever the screaming boy moves it seems the dog already knows and moves as well, blocking him, knowing and intending something bad, otherwise why do what it's doing—

* * * *

That same morning, Emma wakes smelling something. It isn't unpleasant to her, but it does not belong in the house. She trots from the bedroom, into the kitchen. Madame is seated at the table. She hasn't made coffee and is not dressed for gardening. This is odd, seeing her still in her nightgown. The smell comes from the counter.

"A beautiful pork roast, ruined. I knew we were going out. I still put it in the oven. I must have pressed a garlic clove. I salted it, I used the pepper mill. I never set the timer, or turned it on. I don't remember any of it. There it's been for three whole days, ruined."

She gets up slowly, goes to the counter and reaches into the cabinet where Emma's food is kept. She brings down a can, puts it in the opener and pushes the button. She takes it away and begins spooning food into Emma's dish. "I don't remember any of it. They found out about the tickets, how I don't know. They said I could hurt someone. A child, a pregnant woman. It's true, I could. What then?"

It is enough to hear the tone of her voice to know Madame is worried. She puts the bowl down. "Ken has power of attorney, that's just common sense for someone my age. He wouldn't do anything selfish. Not on his own, anyway."

Emma eats. Her habits are much less coarse than Bill's. Often, she leaves much of what is there, coming back later. Madame watches her. "Without the car, I don't see how I can stay here," she says. "I told them I wouldn't consider it without you. They said that wouldn't be a problem, they know places that take dogs."

Emma goes on eating, concentrating on her food. Madame's voice is not so serious now. "A child, Emma. Or a pregnant woman. But I just hate the idea, I've seen those places. The best of them are so sad. Little outings to the mall. Seniors Day at the zoo. Song fests, people with no talent brought in to play the organ. Magicians, faith healers."

She looks down as Emma moves to her water dish. "I suppose there comes a time. I'd just rather it were later than sooner."

* * * *

"What's up, old timer? What did you do now?"

The garage door is rolling up. Bill's tail bangs the parked car as the mister drives his golf cart in. He comes to a stop. "Why'd she put you out here?"

"Ron's crying."

The son swings off the cart and walks to the entrance. The door closes as Vinyl turns off the motor. "I hope you didn't pee again. That does *not* go over." He gets out, Bill waiting for the mister to enter the house before him. The missus had come running, the stepmother standing on the grassy slope with the baby, calling, It's all right, Ronnie, everything's all right! Reaching the boy, the missus knelt and held him, smoothing his back, hugging him. Leading him by the hand, she had then grabbed Bill's collar and pulled him with surprising strength across the fairway, up the incline. Bad dog, she kept saying. Stupid mutt.

Inside, the crying is louder, coming from the parents' room. Having given the baby to the missus, the stepmother is trying to comfort the boy. She is ignorant of what took place as she and the missus ate coffee cake at the neighbor's. She can't know that, however fearful he might have been, Ronald is now exploiting the moment. In fact, his fear of the dog ended seconds after the missus held him. He broke off crying to have a frozen fudge bar, but then resumed it in anticipation of his father's return, to ensure his sister would get what she deserves for having refused to insert the *Toy Story* DVD.

It's working. The Game Boy has been taken away, and there will be no TV for the rest of the day. And no pool.

No, not a good day. But the mister never fails with *dinner*, always feeding Bill before the family eats. It isn't necessary. The dog never bothers people at mealtimes the way dogs often do—dogs that sidle up to the table and make the rounds, being needy, pleading, sometimes even trained by foolish masters to sit and smile for tidbits.

No. Bill always lies beneath the table where he belongs. Or, like tonight, he watches from the living room, sprawled on the cool tile as voices rise and fall. Perhaps this night he has some small sense of absence, of something missing. They are all there except the baby. She is back in the parents' room, asleep in her cradle. But Ruby is silent. Other times at meals she talks a lot, telling her father every detail she can think of, anything to hear his voice and glow in the warmth of his gaze. Tonight, like Bill earlier, she is "in the doghouse" for not watching her brother. She is being very quiet.

After dinner, weather permitting between the meal and final walk of the day, Bill is allowed to go outside for an hour. Occasional lapses notwithstanding, everyone but the missus knows he's a "good" dog—that is, one that doesn't dig—not often—or bark, or make messes on other residents' property. A vague understanding has developed among dog owners in this part of Donegal that their pets gather at this time, and that the socialization is good for them. It is known the dogs find each other—behind this lanai, under a certain cabbage palm. Club rules forbid it, but as long as there are no complaints, what's the harm?

Tonight, they are lying on a grassy plot behind Madame's. It feels protected, the space sheltered by a grouping of three pygmy date palms. But no Emma.

—She was at the window yesterday, Chiffon says.

—She's in there right now, Luger tells her.

Bill looks, seeing the poodle before the doorwall. She is plump and brown, her long ears hanging in a way that just now makes her narrow muzzle look more pointed. He feels a kinship with her because of her size and color, because she accepts him the way Hotspur does. Meeting them on walks, he has seen how strange other poodles seem. They're white like Chiffon, but shorn and shaved at the groomer's to look like topiary. Not Emma. She is trimmed, but no shrub.

Tonight, though, she looks—he doesn't know how—different. Behind her just now, the mistress passes, dressed in one of the long things his own missus wears in the morning. She moves slowly, not looking out. *Madame*, they call her. Her neighbors picked up the name from her mister and still use it on the street. Madame, hello, Madame, you're looking well. Emma adores her the way Bill worships Vinyl. Whenever Madame passes her dog, she never fails to touch her curly, lamb-like back. But not tonight. This, perhaps, is why Emma, still looking out at them, seems different.

—Where's Hotspur? he asks.

—Does he come out? Chiffon sneezes. —I can't remember.

—He has a territory, Luger says. Two houses. His border is two houses in either direction. Then he stops.

—What is territory? Do I have territory?

—You are a companion breed. Your work is to look a certain way, and be with with your missus all the time.

—I don't understand.

Luger doesn't know many words. But he has a good memory and respects this quality in other dogs. Emma's memory is big, like Hotspur's. Even so, Luger would be surprised to learn of a newspaper story about a border collie named Rico. Tested for what is called "fast mapping," Rico was told a word and asked to pick out an object from among fifty things. Knowing the names of the other forty-nine objects, he found the fiftieth in one try. Chiffon has never given evidence of remembering anything but the brand names of dog treats.

Bill turns to listen. The sound is coming from the end of the cul de sac.

—Hear him?

—Hotspur? Chiffon sneezes.

—His mistress went somewhere, Luger says. —The woman who works the vacuum is taking care of him. I saw the car.

—It's bad, Bill says. —He's going crazy. He says Cliff Gilmore is at the beach. My mister walked us and Hotspur ran off.

—I think my mistress talked about that, Chiffon says.

She raises a paw and puts it back. She has had a thought. Luger looks at her, then at Bill. He does not feel any closeness to the big mongrel, but for just a second the two dogs share a moment of surprise.

* * * *

Back home, Bill finds the mister and his son watching TV. In the master bedroom, a small second set on the dresser has a built-in DVD player. It is playing the movie about pigs, one of Ronald's favorites. He is sprawled on his stomach on the bed, watching intently. Bill goes back to the front of the house. The missus and her new daughter-in-law are still at the dining table. They are talking about the new house being built outside Philadelphia. It won't be ready until September. While dad goes back and forth to England to do his job—something related to fiber optics—Ronald and Ruby will divide their time between their mother's co-op apartment in Brooklyn Heights, and the grandparents' Michigan lake house, with their new stepmother and the baby.

Tired of lying on the hard tile floor in the kitchen, Bill goes back to the TV room to be with the mister. Vinyl isn't there now, just the son.

Always alert to sounds inside the house and out, Bill hears a rhythmic, scratchy noise. He looks in the children's room. Empty. The sound is coming from the parents' room. The door is ajar. He pushes with his paw—it's dark. Ruby is on the bed, on her back. One hand is rocking the baby cradle next to her, the source of the sound. It's one of Ruby's jobs, to rock the cradle this way until the baby stops crying or falls asleep. As Bill comes in she looks over. "Hello, dog. Thanks a lot."

Rocking the cradle, she looks again at the ceiling. Bill stands at the entry, waiting for more words. The mister always says more, his voice rising and falling. Even the missus. She has never liked him, but even she talks to Bill when no one's around. Her voice is different at such times, softer, even friendly. But here and now there is something not right about it. The girl should be with the boy, or taking Bill for the nightly walk. He will be fine now. What happened before was wrong, and he knows it. He was dragged by the missus and scolded, put in the garage. The punishment happened close enough to the offense so that the two were connected in his mind. It registered and he understood—no more herding.

"Cra—dle, cra—dle, cra—dle—"

Staring up, Ruby keeps moving her arm. "Cra—dle, cra—dle—" She looks over and Bill steps closer. She is saying it for him, and he waits for a command, for something more. "Crad—dle, Cra—dle—" She is saying it slowly, keeping time with the swing, still speaking and working it as she again raises both her legs, the way she did that morning, eyes on him, showing him again how she can balance that way with long legs like her dad's, legs, he told her, that meant she would turn out to be a long drink of water.

But without both hands flat on the bed, it doesn't work long. The weight of her now topples away on the mattress. Bracing for balance, Ruby forgets the cradle and shoves down. It dips sharply, losing its load and righting, swinging freely. The baby is crying. Ruby rolls to her right and scrambles around the bed. Bill backs away and barks. It's wrong what has happened, the baby smell meaning to be careful and watchful. He barks again as Ruby gathers up her baby brother. The door bangs open.

"What the hell—"

"It's not me, daddy, I didn't do anything."

"What happened here?" She is holding and rocking it as the stepmother and missus come in. "I'm asking you a question, Ruby. *What happened?*"

"I was just rocking him, I was on the bed—"

"Do you know what might've happened if this floor wasn't carpeted? What if you were on the lanai?"

"It's all right—" The stepmother comes to Ruby and takes the baby. "That's all right, isn't it? That's all right—"

"I'm asking you a question."

"Bill."

"What about Bill?"

"He did it with his paw. He put a paw on the swing. I tried to stop him, he snapped at me."

"Why didn't you say something?"

"It happened so fast. I think he wanted the baby."

"My God—" The missus steps to the mother and looks down at the baby.

"Come on, Bill—"

Having just entered, the mister steps forward and takes the dog by the collar. Why? I barked to warn you, Bill thinks being pulled. You came as you should, to help the new pack member, the whelp. I'll go anywhere, he thinks, being dragged toward the garage entrance. Anywhere you want, always. What did I do?

The Martini Laugh

"It's not as though I don't know what to do. I thought about it often enough, after Archie died. Check the pool-service schedule. The day they're due, tie Archie's bowling bag good and tight to my belt. With a knot I can't change my mind about and untie. Carry it out here and jump. It's fitting, don't you think? This nice pool he loved so much, with his ball? Knowing there wouldn't be all that unpleasantness about being found days later. Just the usual clucking over someone taking matters into her own hands. That way, they wouldn't have lots of sordid details to work with. That would frustrate some of them."

Madame smiles to herself. They are on the lanai. Usually, she has her evening martini during the news, but tonight she is stretched out on a chaise, balancing the tall cocktail glass on her stomach. Emma lies at her side. Clear and full of color, the deservedly famous Naples sunset is underway. Puffy clouds roam and change color like a slow-motion kaleidoscope. Under the covered part of the lanai, a ceiling fan turns. It's warm but not so humid this evening. Madame's work in the flower beds outside the cage is now being rewarded. This *payoff* as she calls it happens every year with the start of rainy season. That's when her ixora and gardenia bushes bloom continuously.

Emma does not know the words—*schedule, bowling, fitting,*

clucking—but she can tell Madame feels less depressed. After finding the roast, she didn't speak all day. Now, with the martini, she is doing what reassures Emma most about her mistress—thinking out loud.

" 'Full of high sentence, but a bit obtuse.' *Think* about jumping, yes. But do it? I'd never have the strength to move the moment to its crisis, plain and simple. And I have to tell you something—" Madame takes a sip. "I'm just the slightest bit curious. I know what it will be like, but there's always something. Not enough, but something. The staff. Some other residents with most of their marbles. Their stories." She laughs and takes another sip. "I'll hear those stories over and over, needless to say. My friend Myrtle Stennis said she was the brain trust at her place. The same people asked her a dozen times a day what day it was. And the time. She died last October. We would have made a good team."

Yes, Madame feels better. It is evident in her laugh. The poodle relaxes and lies flat. "They say they'll take good care of you. At first, his wife tried telling me assisted living accepted dogs your size. I told her I knew better. 'Oh, well, then, Lydia, she'll come live with us.' "

Madame drinks her drink. She sighs and balances the glass. No longer in her nightgown, she is wearing a wrap skirt and one of Archie's white dress shirts. She still has them laundered, wearing them with his cuff links, even though they're frayed.

"That's really the most irritating thing. She thinks because I'm slipping I don't know anything at all. Most of the friends I still have went to assisted living long ago. Where does she think I was headed when I got those tickets? No, Emma. You're not the assisted-living type. You're too much dog, that's the problem. We have to hope my son has some backbone. If he doesn't, I'd hate to do it, but wills can be changed."

Nature vs Nurture

It confuses him, being on the lead again. That never happens anymore, not even when Ruby walks him. He knows I obey, Bill thinks, walking on the mister's left as always. Why put it on?

It is night, streetlamps making the buzzing sound, haloed by bugs. He looks up at one as the missus talks. Again this afternoon he was put in the garage, hearing them on the other side of the door, talking, talking. At such times he wishes he were smarter. Emma would know, he thinks. Know what they want, what I have to do.

All he wants on this night at the beginning of June, walking the still-warm pavement with the mister and missus, is to be the best dog. What else is there? What's life but doing right and getting scratched for it, just the right way? Fed well, walked, waiting for the clap and then jumping into the pool, the lake?

Nothing else. Herding the boy made Ronald cry, but how could you think I mean harm? Me? Your own dog? To even think of harming anyone with the pack scent? Or those who come to the house and shake hands, touch faces with their mouths? That is always tense, but he's learned not to worry. It's greeting behavior, like smelling anus or nose.

"You're really getting carried away."

Vinyl tries to put his arm around the missus. "No." She has her own arms folded, marching the way she does when angry. He knows that much, she's mad. At you, he thinks. Every now and then she looks down at him. What is it? Bill wonders. Trotting easily, healthy and comfortable in his now fully grown body, he is picking up all the tension in the missus' walk, her stiffness. She has never stayed mad so long. She complains about shedding and the rare accident, the almost non-existent lapses when something *demands* digging. It's the bad thing under the bed, he thinks, marching, needing now to pee but sensing that this walking, this marching serves some human demand in the mister and missus to move as they argue. But the really bad part is not knowing. If you know, you can do something. Change, fix things, humble yourself with looks and sloped shoulders, slumping away and flopping down so they can see you feel awful. Like death.

"They'll be with us at the lake for weeks. Months. It's just not right. You have to see that."

"One time."

"I just don't understand you. '*One* time.' You act like you *know* this can't happen again. You know no such thing."

"I know the dog."

"Oh, is that right?"

"Yes, that's right. Isn't it, Bill? You wouldn't hurt that baby. You messed up with a paw. We'll make sure you aren't around the cradle. Problem solved."

"Problem solved, just like that. Ruby said he snapped."

"Ruby was scared. She was responsible, just talking. Her dad comes in—"

"Just talking."

"Stop repeating what I say, I don't like it."

"You're not supposed to like it." The missus takes out a handkerchief and blows her nose. She has allergies that get worse in warm weather. She puts the handkerchief back in her shorts pocket. "There's something in the paper all the time about this sort of thing. Every week. Terrible, terrible stories."

"Sensational crap. Rottweilers and pit bulls. Anyone lets those things near children ought to be horsewhipped."

"But not old Bill. As if you know anything about him."

"Honey—"

"Don't honey me, this is serious. You *don't* know anything. You say he's a Lab mix. That's nice. What else? You don't know what's going on in that big dog's head."

Yes, she's still mad. Bill wants even more to stop and pee, wants now to defecate but he keeps trotting at the mister's side, yearning for the lamppost ahead but not yet, wanting to be good.

"The little male dachshund. Wolfi. He bit a child at a birthday party."

"Jesus. 'The little male dachshund.' They're all little."

"I'm not letting this go. This is serious."

Someone is calling. "Well, hello there—"

The missus' voice has changed. Chiffon's owner steps into the light of the streetlamp. Trust Fund, Madame calls her. The mister and missus stop to wait for her. Having to pee and defecate, Bill sits. The woman is walking alone, shoes clacking the way he remembers. She is shiny in places on her arms and neck. As she nears, shiny things dance from her ears, the way Emma's ears flap when she trots.

"Isn't it a beautiful night?"

"Beautiful. Nice to see you."

"Pretty soon, them skeeters will be out in full force. I thought I better take advantage."

"Where's Chiffon?" The mister takes off his hat and holds it behind him.

"Do dogs get colds?" Trust Fund stops before them. "I suppose they do. I got out her leash, I said, 'Let's go.' That's all it ever takes. She just looked at me and sneezed. 'Okay,' I told her. '*Be* that way.' "

It is too much, he can't wait longer. Bill pulls the mister. "Excuse us—" He trails after, dragged toward the streetlamp.

The woman laughs. "I bet Bill rules the roost in your house. Such a nice dog."

"Not if you have to clean up after him."

"The storm? I know. Chiffon cried through the whole thing. But she was good."

"Have you seen Glenda Gilmore?"

"Actually, I called there tonight. I thought she might want to get out. She's up in Cleveland, seeing to things. I don't know if the cleaning woman's reached her yet."

"Something's wrong?"

"You haven't heard? Well, no, you wouldn't have. I just learned it myself, from the cleaning woman. She's at the house hoping he'll come back. The dog ran off this morning. Hotsie?"

"Hotspur. Oh God. Glenda doesn't need that now. We knew how upset he was. Border collies get so attached—"

Finished now, Bill lifts his leg as the mister uses the plastic bag. *Hotspur*, he heard the word. And again. Still he pees. Where is the collie? Was the Gilmore woman out tonight walking him, are they walking right now? Coming this way, on the median? Bill hopes so. He looks up the street, but sees nothing. Hotsie is smart. Bill lowers his leg, sure the collie knows what to do.

He and the mister walk back to the sidewalk. "—torn all to pieces. She had to throw out slipcovers, he knocked over a piece of Steuben glass."

"They're very high strung. They need a lot of exercise. Cliff used to give him that every day."

"Glenda would be devastated. First Cliff, then his dog."

"Oh I'm sure he'll come back." Trust Fund adjusts her bracelets. "He's out on the town is all."

"I hope you're right. When she first met Cliff, he already had

Hotsie. She always said she had two husbands. One Englishman, one Scotsman."

Bill keeps looking, hoping Hotspur will step from darkness into the cone of bluish light humming down from the next streetlamp. He looks back to the house where the collie lives. Lights are on. Looking at them, he hears the mister and missus making final sounds. Now he takes his place and they walk in silence. When Trust Fund's shoes are gone, they are talking again.

"I was looking at what?"

"I suppose men like it."

"Like *what?* What are you talking about?"

"You know what I'm saying. Men like the flashy type."

"What difference does it make? It's her thing. She's alone, it gives her pleasure. What's the problem?"

Whatever it means Bill hears this a lot—*What's the problem.* The mister's voice always goes up at the end.

"In the middle of the night, out for a walk. You'd think she was on her way to Mardi Gras." Vinyl doesn't answer. "She doesn't go to the husband's memorial service, but she calls the widow when her dog's sick. So she won't have to walk alone."

When the mister sighs, Bill looks up. His face was like that earlier, before the woman, when the missus kept saying *baby*. "I'm right. That's the only reason she called. So someone would see her latest getup."

"You're getting catty." Bill's ears mark the word. "First the dog, now the glitter queen, as you call her."

"I'm not leaving it alone about the dog. It's too important."

No, Bill thinks. No Hotspur. Not tonight.

Bait and Switch

Two days pass with more leaps into the pool. Bill makes them with special gusto, grateful to be forgiven by the boy. Ronald throws the ball and cheers when Bill hits the water. He braces on the deck, pulling the rope.

And Ruby. She is very nice to him, using the brush on his back as he sits for her. This is one of the best things, the brush. The mister showed her how, Ruby kneeling next to Bill on the deck, smoothing the stiff bristles along his sides. But she isn't allowed now to walk him. That's over. And he is kept sometimes in the garage, hearing the baby inside. At least the mister has stopped using the lead. Bill does his best to do everything right, to not run ahead, or chase geckos. When other dogs and owners approach, he stays at Vinyl's side.

And then the son and his family are gone. The house is silent. Bill walks through the rooms, ears alert, still smelling them. No baby or second woman talking in the kitchen to the missus. No chicken video or Cartoon Network. It's almost *too* quiet. Over the last two weeks he has come to like the action in the house, the extra walks and exercise.

But all of it will happen soon again, at the lake. After the car trip. He doesn't exactly know this from last summer, but has a sense of continuity based on the mister, and water. Not as people do, but it's dimly present in his mind, without time sense but real enough. Odors bring it to him. When Vinyl makes a certain meal on the grill, the dog thinks of the Michigan beach, he doesn't know why. They were all of them there—the son, Ronald and Ruby. But not the wife and baby. They are new. Or when the mister puts on one of the videotapes he made. He did this the day after the family left. "Check yourself out, Bill—" Hearing his name as he drank water in the kitchen, the dog trotted out, finding Vinyl in the TV room. "That's you—" he pointed the remote. It was him, on the screen. He didn't recognize himself, but a dog was standing under trees, just behind the log house in Michigan, looking up a pine and barking.

Quiet yes, but a lot is going on. Suitcases have been brought down from the attic. Serving dishes the missus uses in both houses are being wrapped in newspaper and put in boxes. There are telephone calls and final visits from Donegal friends. He is no longer being allowed out after dinner. He whines until the missus scolds.

For this reason, he doesn't know Hotspur is dead.

Glenda Gilmore, still in Cleveland, got the call from Terasita, her housekeeper. The woman was very apologetic. He just run out, I don't got no chance to grab him, I real sorry, it just happen. Back the next morning, Glenda didn't come directly from the Fort Myers airport. She drove straight to the beach, searching the route she and her husband had always taken with the dog. Then to Naples, north to Lowdermilk Park. Exhausted from the summer heat, she went to the house, changed clothes, and resumed her search. Now south to the last point of Naples public beach access, in Port Royal at 33rd Street. Then north. She asked at hotels and condo complexes, at chickee bars. People shook their heads. Two men offered to help look with her if they could first buy her a drink. At Clam Pass, the afternoon heat dangerous in the dense mangrove swamp, instead of taking the tram to the beach, she walked the length of the boardwalk. Running her hand along the rail, Glenda looked down into the coiled hoops of mangrove roots. At the beach, she drank a bottle of Evian and asked everyone there. He's black, she told them. With white markings on his chest and paws. Very friendly, you'd remember. She walked to the estuary and back, feeling lightheaded. Back in the parking lot, she sat a quarter of an hour in Cliff's Explorer, crying now, feeling sick and desperate. Then Vanderbilt Beach. There was so much beach in Naples, ten miles. Realizing then that there was no reason to think Hotspur hadn't gone farther north, to Bonita Beach, she felt hopeless. She drove home, called the Naples police, the Collier County Sheriff's Department—even the Lee County sheriff's office, giving the description.

Public Works landscapers spreading mulch found Hotspur on the Davis Boulevard median (she had passed the body without seeing, talking to Cliff as she drove, asking what she should do). He'd been struck by a car or pickup as he tried crossing, running for the beach where Cliff Gilmore was waiting with the Frisbee, in his shorts, standing in the lap of water, very tan and the hair on his arms bleached as white as the collie's chest.

All of this tumbled out of her on Madame's lanai later that afternoon. You're the only woman here who doesn't treat me like a hooker, she said. Like a tramp. I'm so sorry, Madame said. People can be pointlessly mean.

But Bill doesn't know.

Nor do Wolfi and Stanzi. Not that such self-absorbed dogs would remember. They are almost never allowed out, but the night the mister is loading the car, they waddle to a stop outside the Vinyls' pool cage. Bill gets up and comes over. —It's wrong, Wolfi says, communicating with his narrow tail and sharp eyes as Bill stops at the screen. The male dachshund is black with brown markings, and this somehow makes him look more forceful. Stanzi is a soft chestnut color. —Wrong, Wolfi repeats.

—Where are the others? Emma? Hotspur?

—We don't go back, Stanzi says in Dog, ignoring the question. —We must be staying. We should leave by now. Something is wrong.

—She's right, Wolfi says —This heat, I don't like it. I hear them talking, they say it's like this all summer. It's not like this where we go. We never stay here. We're supposed to go in the plane, in the bag thing.

—Like always, Stanzi says.

—Our mister and missus are fighting all day now. They don't have us up for television—

—They ignore us. They don't play golf—

—No cart rides, nothing, Wolfi says. —It's wrong. What is it? Is something wrong here, too?

—We're leaving. Soon. They have the boxes and my crate.

—What can we do? Stanzi asks. —It's not right, we're nervous.

—She threw up this morning, Wolfi says. —In the laundry room. From nerves. The missus was crying, doing laundry. She never does laundry. Stanzi just threw up.

It goes on like that, the two dachshunds repeating themselves, shifting and pacing outside the cage until their mister calls. —It's not right, Stanzi says again. She turns away and the male follows. —This heat. I feel sick.

Dachshunds are courageous, fearless even, given their size. But they don't handle change well. That explains the friend of a grandchild who was nipped at a birthday party last year. Bill knows none of it. He wishes to see the other dogs. It's part of his schedule, something he anticipates. He waits until after dark before giving up. He paws the closed glass doorwall, clicking his nails. The mister lets him in.

He says nothing, looking down. For several days he's been this way, stroking Bill's head in the usual way. He does this now, silently. "All right, old timer, let's go." Bill trots through the house, waiting and ready when Vinyl opens the front door.

* * * *

The next morning, he knows everything to do. There's the walk, just a quick one to the end of the street before eating. He gulps his food as the missus puts away dishes and rattles silverware. They always take his bowls in the car, putting them down at rest stops and the motels that accept dogs. He hears his name mentioned. Each time the mister pats Bill, they look at each other. Something is wrong. Bill can tell from the eyes, even the smell, something acidic and different that has to do with how the missus is not talking this morning. All week they talked, voices rising in sharp exchanges he wished would end. Then nothing, like this.

Otherwise, everything is the same. The mister goes all through the house rattling windows, checking controls on the wall. He turns off the hot water tank, puts down ant traps and goes up on the ladder to lock the garage attic. The missus long ago emptied the refrigerator. The last thing the mister does is to circle the exterior of the house, pulling down hurricane shutters over each window and door.

At last they all go out the front. The mister slams the door, uses his key, then a remote to lower the last roll-down metal shutter. The missus is already seated when he steps to the back of the van. He opens the tailgate, then the cage. "Okay, Bill—" Up and in he goes in a single motion, turning and lying down as the wire door is fastened shut. Where are the bowls? The mister always puts them in the cage. The tailgate comes down, and this, too, is confusing. The last thing is for the mister to turn the cage, facing front. A door slams. The motor starts. They are backing down the drive. Bill's bulky body shifts as the van turns onto Donegal Boulevard. The tailgate window blinks and flashes with tops of trees. There are other turns, words spoken to the guard at the gatehouse. Bill is waiting for the hum and soft vibration of tires at highway speed, the lulling, sleepy limbo between stops—

None of this happens. Lying in the crate, head erect, he remains alert. Not worried, curious. Like people, dogs have to adapt but are less well suited to it, more comfortable with routine, with mission and duty. But why worry? You're with the mister, Bill thinks, swaying in the cage. The best mister, the ultimate good thing that makes the days one after another move ever farther from memory traces that sometimes take the place of treed squirrels in his dreams—the mill evil of overbred bitches and sick, undersized puppies removed from the litter. Then escape. In some sense, Bill does think of it. Gently swayed, in some sense he recalls the tics and chiggers sapping his strength, finally forcing choice, compelling him to decide that this one on the road, his smell, manner of walk, his daily passage and eyes make him the one to act on, the one to step from the pine forest and follow—

They have stopped. The door slams on the mister's side, not the missus'. It's confusing. Time should pass, the lull of the road at high speed. He doesn't need a walk, it isn't time to eat. The beach? When the tailgate opens, it isn't the beach smell, but there are many odors, some of them alarming, familiar. The mister opens the crate and snaps on the lead.

"Come on, old timer—" He hears them, balks and braces but is pulled down onto warm asphalt—other dogs. Wrong, he thinks, legs stiff, being dragged. Not a rest stop, not where we sleep. Instead, dogs, their smell of fear and fatigue, smells of bleach, medicine, food, feces—He sits down, still being dragged. "Don't, Bill, come on, dog..."

Someone is holding open a door. The smells blow out, full of barking and scents of big animals bred and trained to be angry. The vet's? He hates going, this is like that but different. Worse. The floor inside feels cold. Cement, not tile like the vet—and no woman is coming to him saying, Hi there, Bill, before getting down to look in his eyes, using her voice to calm him—

Someone else. As the mister holds the lead, someone else is putting a thing over Bill's head, over his muzzle. Stronger than the mister, he is pulling now, dragging the powerful dog across the floor. Another door opens—the sound deafening. When it slams closed, still being dragged he tries to bay for the mister, thinks he can hear him through the chaos of barking. Crazed eyes glare at him from stacks of cages. Teeth flash. In other cages, dogs lie motionless, heads on the floor looking out without seeing. He is put in a crate the size of the mister's but not the same—wire underfoot. Whining, trying to bark but prevented by the thing on his head, he watches the strange someone-else looking in at him. It is very bright. For an instant, where he is makes sense to him— from the sharp, yellow light in front of him, on the cement floor. The pool deck. No. This is no deck, this is just one thing. You know what it is, he thinks. You know everything about it. Why are you here? What have you done? The bad thing, herding the boy—but those things are so far back they can't explain this. In the fetor of dog hysteria and defeat—he can't make sense of it.

Nor can Fred Vinyl, already traveling north on the Interstate. Escaping, really. Doing eighty-five to be done with it, Vinyl wants to put distance between cause and effect. All *he* knows is that she insisted. The cradle business set her off. Silent behind the wheel, feeling hot even in the blast of cold hair blowing from the dashboard, he believes she has used it. Exploited one thing to accomplish a long-standing goal. Married forty-four years next January, he still cares for his wife in the growing-old manner of need and routine, the thought of which when young and first married seemed boring and defeated. Now it suits him. So, he yielded, holding out a while, but at some point coming to see it wouldn't work, not this time, not for this thing.

Darkness at Noon

It's a test, he decides. Something to do with obedience training.

When the stranger comes back, he squats down and studies Bill for several seconds. "You're a big dude, but your guy's right. You're a pussycat."

The voice sounds calm, not angry. The man opens the cage and takes off the muzzle. Bill whines. This one's smell is all wrong, but you have to trust people. Small, big, men or women, children—that's how it is. Even here, in this place that just now is bringing to life unwanted memories and feelings from his first awful year, Bill stretches his head to be touched. This one scratches him under the chin, almost the right way. It's reassuring, familiar. Except the smell—

And noise. A cloud of sensations crowds in from all directions. It sets Bill barking. He tries to shove out of the cage. "No, you don't, sport—" The man pushes the cage door shut against the dog's weight, holds it there with his hip until the catch is in place, then leaves. Bark, Bill thinks. That's what you do here. What else is there? So, he barks, filling his big chest over and over, the sound joining others.

Loud and brittle in early-afternoon sun streaming through a skylight, the barking is not from pampered lap dogs meeting under a streetlamp as their owners debrief each other on the day's golf or tennis game, this one's cocktail party, that one's grandchildren—the surgeries, the oxygen delivery man who always brings treats for dogs, the pool girl all the wives voice sympathy for but actually prefer because she has a prosthetic leg.

No. Here, along with dogs whose owners have died or gone to nursing homes, or dogs who just wandered away and will likely be collected soon, are dogs either given up in the right way, or dumped on roads and at rest stops, at gas stations. Some were inconveniences, dogs that on second thought seemed a bad idea. Others threatened children and postal workers. Some dogs here have sent people to the hospital. Not the thief trying to remove the wall safe in Mel's Marine, or the one who forgot his bolt cutter when he dropped himself inside the chain-link fence at the BMW dealership—other people. People just out walking, people delivering fliers or pizzas—people who couldn't know that the dog in the too-small yard or all-wrong one-bedroom apartment were bred and then trained to patrol a perimeter, a territory. People who weren't known pack members of such a dog's owner.

In their way, such dogs are no different from border collies or Labs or willful West Highland terriers digging for China in the garden. They are just fulfilling their mission, but a mission incompatible with circumstances. Such dogs belong on farms or ranches. Otherwise, their territories spread to include other yards and streets, even other neighborhoods. In the end, sometimes by owners as reluctant as Bill's, they are brought here.

It's a shelter, a good one. Vinyl called around to be sure. There was no question of anyone at Donegal taking the dog. Why ask? Even knowing better, some residents were still intimidated when Bill rounded the corner. So, an animal rescue shelter. It's not a bad place, of its kind. But to Bill, barking hard in the strange crate, it comes too close to the past. The sound of it, the powerful odors cause him to lose control, defecating and peeing there in the box, something unthinkable in his own crate, empty and rattling in the back of the van as the Vinyls drive north in silence.

During the afternoon, people interested in adoption come to see the dogs. A couple stops to look in. "He's a barker, isn't he?" the woman says.
"We just got him. He'll settle down."
"What's his name?"
"Just Bill."
"Bill."
"The owner said it had to do with a song."
The woman keeps looking in. Her husband has moved on to the next cage. "*That's* not very inspired," she says. "I'd name a dog like that King or Titan."
"He's big, but his bio looks good."
"Or Czar Nicholas. Something appropriate."
"He belonged to a couple on a golf course."
"You're kidding. We live on a golf course. They'd never let anyone keep a dog like that. I bet that's why they had to give him up."
She moves on. Some time later, a different stranger brings food. It's not his kind, but the bowl is Bill's. The water dish, too. It confuses and elates him to eat and drink in this strange place from his own heavy stone bowls. The mister brought them from the lake, to replace the stainless steel bowls Bill kept tipping over.

The skylight softens. More people come. A woman interested in "something that likes airplanes" shuffles down and back with a walker. Then another couple. "We want a real dog," the man says stopping. "Like that. None of these little toy deals."
" 'We.' You mean 'I.' We have a new baby, now he wants a dog. It's psychological, isn't it? Do you see that happening? People have a baby and the man all at once wants a dog? I'd like to know."
"Actually," says the stranger who brought the food, "yes, we do. That one's a nice dog. He was well treated and trained, but he's probably not for you. He tipped over a cradle."

It grows dark. A light bulb shines somewhere, but before him it is blue, from the moon. He can see eyes opposite, hear dogs sigh. It's a test, he keeps thinking. Obedience training. But it's time for the walk now. He'll be here for that, he wouldn't forget that, he never forgets. That's our way, Bill thinks. That's what we do, every night. Then we go home in the van. If there's a storm, they won't leave this time, they'll stay and everything they want from the best dog—that's what I'll be.

* * * *

"We just crossed the state line. We're in Georgia now. How long do you plan to keep the silent treatment going?"

Vinyl doesn't answer. At the last stop, he removed the noisy crate and left it behind a gas station.

"We have to eat. Aren't you hungry? Aren't you going to talk to me the whole way?"

When he still doesn't answer, she reaches down to the bag of CDs. It's how she's dealt with the trip, filling up the silence. She straightens in her seat. They have already listened to the complete Golden Oldies anthology—five disks—and the first part of a Patricia Cornwell novel. The missus found the story boring and stopped it just north of Gainesville.

"How long are you intending to punish me?"

"I'll talk to you when I'm good and ready."

Usually, they share the driving, alternating in two-hour shifts. Today he is doing it all. Somehow, it's a matter of honor, male pride. He agreed to do something wrong, he betrayed a trust. The longer they've been on the road, the more convinced he's become that his mistake reveals a profound falling off from his true self. At some point he thought of Cliff Gilmore. He felt ashamed, cowardly. Cliff would never have done it, Vinyl thought.

He has not actually felt old to himself until now. Older, yes.

He *is* old. Let them talk all they want about this new diet, that vitamin supplement—seventy is old. He pops Advil tablets now like they're peanuts, he stuffs himself with oat and wheat bran. His prostate must be the size of a muskmelon. But he has not actually *felt* old until now. It's Bill, he thinks. You betrayed him.

"We'll get something else." His wife says this in her kindest voice. "I understand, Fred. I really do. I know a dog's important to you. But this was just not meant to be. We'll get something smaller. A bichon."

"So you can decorate it? Trick it out with little hats?"

After a moment, she turns away, looking out her side window.

Time passes. Days. Dogs have no strong sense of it, but the light comes and goes. More people visit. He is allowed out in a fenced yard for exercise. Once, a rottweiler, abandoned at a convenience store attacked him. Hardly knowing what he did, Bill fought back until someone came with a pole, a loop on the end, and dragged the rottweiler away.

Beyond the yard's high cyclone fencing he sees other buildings, utility sheds. Heavy equipment comes and goes. On the far side of the buildings he can see undergrowth. It looks no different from the jungle rough on the far side of the eleventh fairway. He starts eating, the food different but good. Still he lunges each mouthful into his throat, gulping until the bowl is empty before lapping water.

People adopt some of the dogs. Other dogs, either too old or vicious are taken out and don't come back.

—Do you understand?

This Dog message comes from eyes in the cage opposite. They are clear and intelligent, belonging to a German shepherd. Hit by a passing car on 41, he's a purebred, not abandoned, just unlucky. Hobbled but ambulatory, he requires surgery that neither the city of Naples nor Collier County can afford. Nor, so far, any potential foster family.

—Do you understand?

—What?

—You think he's coming back. The dog shifts his muzzle to see Bill better. —Tonight. Tomorrow. You believe that.

Bill does not want to communicate about it with the other dog. He turns away and lies facing the back of the crate. Whatever time means, a lot has gone by. What he now fears is that whatever happened to Cliff Gilmore has happened to the mister. No, impossible. He's fine, Bill thinks. This is part of a class, some special exercise. It should be over by now, but the mister's not here. It happened once before, Bill can't know when. Here in Florida, Vinyl had an angioplasty, and spent two days at the Cleveland Clinic. Those two nights, Cliff Gilmore walked Bill with Hotspur. Then the mister came back. He clapped in the pool, the missus going inside, closing the doorwall to protect her clothes.

Restive, accustomed to more exercise, he works his way around in the cage. When he settles again, there are the intelligent eyes.

—I'm not defeated. The shepherd stands and shakes himself. —I'm not a dog that gives up. Some here quit. They stop eating, sleep all the time. Shepherds aren't like that. They go until they drop. But I know humans.

—What do you want? Bill gets up. The ridge of his spine presses the top of the crate. —I like you. What do you want?

—I like you, too. The shepherd's eyes and noble head express this meaning. —There's shepherd in you. Not much but some.

—He'll come. There are other dogs where he's taking me. Where we live. Maybe you can come, too.

—You live here now. You still don't understand.

The journey home to Michigan takes either two or three days, depending on how they feel. This trip they make in two.

Vinyl didn't talk to his wife until dinner that first night on the road. Sipping his rob roy before the meal, he watched her looking out on the dining room, seeking any alternative to facing him. With the simple pragmatism that characterizes long marriages—that is, the mutual acceptance of deeply flawed human nature—he felt more than thought how much he still cared for his wife, still liked to look at her and hear her voice. So, he brought up neutral topics—chores waiting for them when they got home. Bedding she always aired, landscaping for him. Always there are lots of leaves to tend to, half rotten after the winter snow and spring rains. Seeing her relief and eagerness to talk, he decided to let it go. Perhaps she's right, he thought, and ordered another rob roy. Little kids, babies. She could be right.

But late the following afternoon, bumping along the shaded dirt road to their place, dark with leafy hardwood summer foliage, the mister caught himself looking in the rearview for the dog. When they reached their property, he braked to a stop outside the pole barn. He'd had it built when they bought the house, a big shiny shed of corrugated steel to house the riding mower, the cars and boats. They opened the gate and followed the walkway, he used his key. Everything was where it belonged, a big log house smelling of sap. He walked then to the end of the property, to check the guest cabin. The lake looked higher than last year. That would be good for boating. The service had come and put in the dock, rolling it down the grassy slope.

So, in the following days he does his best. He repairs a broken water line in the irrigation system, gets out a ladder and cleans the gutters. His wife comes out to watch, for safety's sake. He cuts the grass, rolling and swaying in the seat, a ride similar to golf carts. He spreads fertilizer, grills. Life lived without Bill is life as it was before the dog. Workable. The first weekend, a former business partner comes to visit. While the wives go scouring the antique shops and yard sales near Cadillac, the men fish. On the lake they talk about friends who have died, the stock market, notorious clients from the past. The mister doesn't bring up the dog, glad his friend never came during Bill's time.

So, life goes on. Persists. But it's not the same. Against his will one afternoon, sitting in one of the Adirondack chairs on the greensward facing the lake, he understands something modestly profound. He had known it before, but not thought about it. It was the dog's vitality he most valued and now misses. Just that, his simple, direct, pull-out-the-stops approach to everything. You're no baby boomer, he thinks, remembering the dog jumping off the diving platform. No all-organic crap or vitamin supplements to help you live to a hundred. Bill was your tonic.

Odd, how his thoughts wander. Sex, for instance. With the new drug (nothing bogus about *that*, he thinks), the mister still has a token sex life. Notwithstanding the annoyingly coy ads on TV featuring models half his age, the stuff does work. As much as anything, though, having sex for both of them these days serves mostly to confirm it's still possible, that they're still in the game.

What's that got to do with Bill? As he almost never does (selling vinyl siding to builders made him well-to-do, not reflective), he sticks with the question. The size of him, for one thing. That was part of it. Bill's a man's dog. Being able to manage him had been a source of pride. Not that that was ever a problem. Never. The mister shakes his head in confirmation. But if you aren't really driven any longer by testosterone, what remains—you could say what now represents getting it up—is vitality. Being ready for things. Being ready to say hell yes, let's do it, whatever "it" might be, whatever you might otherwise have cancelled or begged off on, asking for a rain check.

The dog gave you more of that, he thinks. Whether it's fair or true he doesn't know, but this conviction leads Vinyl to a second thought. She was jealous of him, he thinks. Your wife was jealous of a damn dog. Jealous, too, of other women, younger ones or those with better figures—especially those younger. Glenda Gilmore, for instance. All that sympathy at the memorial service, when in fact she and almost every woman on the property believes Glenda married Cliff just for money. So what? he thinks, not seeing the lake. What if it's true? Whose business is it?

Still, resenting someone who looks that good, a former model with whom you can't hope to compete in that way—that, too, is understandable. But a dog? A big old mutt? He believes it, though. That night at dinner he is quiet, eating his pork chops and sweet potato, saying nothing. Good or bad, he always compliments his wife's cooking. When he fails to, she tries different topics. He answers, but hardly moves his mouth.

She knows what it is, and eats then in silence. But by the end of the meal, she has managed to convince herself he is coming down with something.

Homeland Security

"Shitfire, that's one big dog."

The stranger sounds young, but has on a cap like the mister's. His face is close to the cage and he is drinking from a cup. Coffee. The mister drinks it in the morning, before the walk. The other man at his side, the stranger who is no longer strange, just wrong, is laughing at whatever the younger man says. The young man stays bent at the waist, looking in.

"I don't want a mean dog. Just a good loud one. It's high crime where I am, you get your break-ins, that stuff. I just thought a good big dog might do the trick."

"This one would definitely make someone think twice."

"That's it, that's just what I'm talking about. All these pit bulls in here, that's plain nuts if you ask me. People say they're all right. Shoot, I figure a pit bull, you're looking at a lawsuit waiting to happen."

"We get a lot of them. It's too bad. They have a place, but not in most people's backyards."

Still the young man keeps looking at him. When this goes on too long, it makes Bill nervous. He turns away and lies facing the back of the crate. "Guess he don't like me."

"They don't like too much eye contact. This one's friendly. His owner gave him up before going back up north."

"Huh. A Yankee dog."

"He lived on a golf course."

"Hell, they wouldn't let some vicious killer dog on one of these courses down here." The other man laughs again. "No, they wouldn't, that's a fact." The two walk away, not down the row of cages but back through the door where the attendants stay. When he settles again facing the bright cone of light coming from the ceiling, the shepherd is looking at him.

—You're leaving. That one's taking you.

—How do you know?

—He stayed at your cage. He stopped looking.

—Do I go back to the golf course? I know that word, I hear it a lot.

—Maybe. This one does something with plastic pipe. Smell it? My owner used that pipe. He did something with it under the sink, in the kitchen. It took a long time, he got angry.

The shepherd is right, on both counts. Dewey Hartman uses a lot of PVC pipe in his work—he installs the circulation systems for swimming pools. Before leaving the shelter, he fills out the paperwork for dog adoption. The next day, he comes back.

—What did I tell you? The shepherd says this with his eyes. Always serious and vigilant, he looks across at Bill with longing.

The man who feeds Bill leads him out on a leash made of chain. Dewey is there with a pickup truck. A crate rests in back. When a hand slaps the truck bed, Bill understands. He jumps up and goes inside.

"Hell, look at that." The young man fastens the door. "Like he knows the whole show."

"He's crate-trained."

"I forgot to ask. Is he housebroke?"

"That, too. He might not respond right away, but the owner

said Bill had some training. Heel, stay, come, lie down. He said the dog's very anxious to please."

The young man looks in again. After a moment, he shakes hands with the attendant, then slams the tailgate. As the truck begins to move, Bill works to keep his balance. The truck bounces more than the van. And it's hot. But to be outside again, away from the kennel—free air fills his lungs. The myriad, rich effects of land and air come to him, rushing, flooding. Soon, he settles down, enjoying the ride.

Two miles east of Collier Boulevard, Dewey turns off Davis, onto a short street of small houses. He pulls in the drive of his rental and brings the truck to a stop. Out and around to the back, he quickly lowers the tailgate. At the shelter, the dog jumped up on his own. He went right inside the crate, borrowed from Dewey's brother. It made the new mister feel good.

"So here we are, Bill." He looks in. "This is my crib."

Crib, cradle. He doesn't remember words the way Emma can, but familiar sounds make him prick up his ears. The crate door opens. "Well, come on, bubba, this is it—" He jumps down and runs to the fence. Lifting his leg, he marks the area. Now he roams, sniffing and urinating as he moves along the cyclone fence. It's a big yard for the size of the house, the shelter requiring fenced yards as a condition of adoption. The young man is laughing. "That's it, Bill, you stake it out. Some clown come in here last month and stole my lawn mower. Right where you are now, give that an extra shot. A nice one from Sears. Hell, I take off ten minutes to Taco Bell, I come back, no more mower. Ain't gonna happen this time, right, Bill? No way."

It gets better. The big yard suits him. There are two live oaks at the back, big ones, and lemon and orange trees the owner planted. But the small house feels cramped to such a big dog. At least Dewey knows enough to move things that might get broken.

The shelter gave him Bill's food and water bowls. He feeds the dog right. But he is not big on walks. Leaving for work early, he leaves Bill in the yard, until a neighbor complains the dog barks. After that, Dewey lets Bill out, then shuts him up. He comes back at noon to eat lunch while the dog is outside. Every few days, he gets the shovel and cleans up.

The new mister has friends at work, other young men who come to the house. They watch sports on Dewey's big TV and drink beer (the mister did this, but at the club, whistling as they walked home). They always go outside and throw the ball in the yard, clapping and cheering as Bill trots back with it, panting but tireless. Or, they take him out in the road and throw it very far. That's best. Once, the new mister and his friends take him to a big park for Frisbee. Hotspur, he thinks, jumping and catching the thing. Maybe he and Cliff are at the beach.

Dogs adjust, and so does Bill. But it's not the same. Traces of the past remain. Left alone all day and sprawled on the kitchen's tile floor, half conscious of dust motes floating in slatted bars of light, Bill senses his inner clock. It still vaguely registers old routines. We should be walking now. Where's the pool? The big ball the son throws in the net? Why isn't the missus talking to me the way she does when the mister leaves to play golf? Where are the other dogs?

Not as good, but a life. Food, some freedom. People two houses away own a dog he never sees. It barks when let out, a high yapping that stops each time a door slams. The mister next door looks over at him when he grills, but doesn't talk. Once, the man's boy, much like Ronald in size and movement, managed to work off the thing on the new mister's gate. The mother saw him from her kitchen window. She slammed out her back door and ran to him, swept him up and ran back inside.

"Good old dog," the new mister says each time he comes back. "Still on the case? That's good, that's your detail." Then he thumps

Bill's broad back, over and over saying "attaboy" like the first mister, but not scratching. Then he goes to the refrigerator, and turns on the TV. No missus lives here. Once, one of them came in late with him. Bill had not been out since dinner. He had almost done the bad thing. He was put in the yard and left there. The hot July air was full of mosquitoes and mites, troubling him as he lay on the cement drive. In the morning, the one-time missus came out and talked to him. Then they were both gone. He's never seen her again.

Lots of people come, each with a special aura, his or her own essence of the human. The owner comes, to make sure her property isn't being damaged by the tenant's new dog. The mister's father comes with his missus. They bring food and sit outside. They all talk the whole time, but not to him. He can't know it, but this missing aspect of his new days tweaks and haunts him. Alone all day, he sleeps most of the time. Awake, he wanders the small rooms looking for the first mister. Looks out windows for him. Listens for the big door going up, for the van or golf cart. He never knew what they were saying, but knew when he was spoken to. And other times when they spoke because of him. Times when he was just there, and, for whatever reason, his presence led them to speak.

One night, the new mister uses the strong scent he wears when he stays out late. He thumps Bill. "Damn, you're a good old dog, that's a fact. You wish me luck, okay? This old boy's way overdue to dip his wick, I can tell you—" He slams the door, and the truck noise slips away.

The windows darken. The new mister keeps a light on in the kitchen. Otherwise, the house is dark. Bill roams. He looks out the front window. Bugs nick the screen, so many now that it's July. Over the weeks he spent in the shelter, several storms battered the place. Lightning flashed down from the skylight. At first he peed and defecated, terrified. But with no bed to squeeze under, no mister, over time he grew indifferent to the pounding. Here, the storms happen daily. Sometimes thunder rumbles for hours but no rain falls. Just now, heat lightning cracks and hides itself. And again.

Leaving the window, he wanders into the new mister's bedroom and flops down. Straightening up earlier, clearing the floor of the week's dirty underwear, Dewey believed these efforts would improve his chances of getting lucky. Bill puts his head down, ears working as thunder rolls and sinks. It has bludgeoned him too often to matter now. He dozes in flashes of heat lightning.

Until the key in the lock.

Up instantly, surprised and delighted he trots to the door leading to the patio. Still it goes on, the key in the lock. He waits. The sound keeps going. He barks. The clicking stops. He barks again, and then it resumes, the agitated skirmishing of metal on metal—and now the door cracks. He has his nose there, knowing already this is not the new mister. He barks, his big voice filling the house—not angry, no watchdog, just barking. A hand tosses something through the crack. It lands behind him, but he keeps his nose in the crack. This time, something drops in front of him. Meat, strong-smelling. He snatches up the jerky and chews. Bill gulps the next strip, not chewing, looking for the next.

This time it's being held in the crack, not dropped. "Be nice, now... No, dog, be nice—"

Bill knows *be nice*. When that's said, you have to calm down and step back, wait a second before the treat comes, or the ball is tossed. You have to *behave*. He backs away from the entry, whining. The strip falls in front of him, he eats. Another. A third. This different mister now steps in and closes the door. He drops another piece of jerky. "See that? All this shit about dogs—" He puts his gloved hand out. Bill noses it. The glove smells of jerky.

"Show me. Go on—" He throws another strip of dry meat.

When Bill has swallowed and looks up, the man says again, "Show me your house, big guy. Go on—"

What does he want? He motions and repeats the sounds. Go somewhere? Into the house? The dog leads him out of the kitchen. "He won't be back. I done the tootsie he's with myself. She's no Britney Spears, but she's in the market. Her place is right around the corner from the bar."

* * * *

Dewey doesn't return until the next morning. He comes in whistling, closes the door, then stops. "Aw, Bill, look what you done—"

Still talking, he tears paper towels, gets down and begins wiping the floor. Bill watches. Too much time has passed for the dog to relate having peed to the mister's scolding. That was after the man left. Just before, he opened the refrigerator and looked in. He found what was left of a key lime pie. Eating out of the pan at the sink, he looked at the dog, and again opened the refrigerator. "Ball Park hot dogs. You could do worse." Throwing the package on the floor, he then carried things outside, coming back twice before he was gone.

The new mister finishes with the towels and throws them in the basket. "But it's not your fault. And let me tell you something, bubba. It was worth a whole lot more grief than this."

But when he goes into the house, his voice rises and falls in anger. He goes all through, kicking furniture, throwing cushions. He throws the TV remote at Bill, then sits facing the empty stand. "Shit. Shit."

His friends come that afternoon. They drink beer and laugh about it. The new mister laughs, too, it's what you do when this happens. "The sucker had some pie and gave Bill there a package of wieners. You can see how it was. Shit, he comes in, he gives Bill here his business card—" The friends are laughing "—'Hey, how they hangin'?' Bill says. 'Whatcha need, some jewelry? Down the hall on the right. How about some high-end electronics? Not a problem, buddy. In the den on your left.'"

Sturm und Drang

—You ran away, the shepherd says. —He hit you?
—No.
—Running is a mistake.
—I didn't run. He was gone all night. I peed. Just once.
—They don't bring you back for that.
—He comes back. He wipes the floor. Everything is all right, then he's yelling. Crazy. Someone came first and took things. A friend. I'm thinking it's all right. He has treats, he gives me food.

Bought originally to guard a furniture store, the shepherd doesn't answer.

Returned to the animal shelter, Bill resumes a life of sordid, empty days. Dogs come and go. Filling the hours, a welter of sensory overload gives way to boredom. Harsh Florida sun hangs all day in front of his crate; at night, shards of lightning stab down through the skylight. Being brought back this way and again confined, he has trouble eating. In four days he loses two pounds.

Then, on the fifth day he is let out in the morning with others, in the fenced yard. Hot and humid, the air is something to push through. By noon the sky has darkened, and by two the trees bordering the adjacent sheds rattle and sway. Dust whips through the yard. A plastic bucket flies against the stucco wall, then a lawn chair. One of the animal-shelter staff is now crossing from the sheds. Hunched and facing away, she is holding on to her broad Smokey-the-Bear hat. As she nears the gate, her phone rings. She unclips it from her belt and starts talking, holding her hat, working to open the gate. The hat blows off. Still talking, she turns and starts chasing it, back toward the sheds. The hat whips and bounces.

The gate bangs open.

—Come on.

The German shepherd is already outside. Skillfully mastering his injured leg, he starts loping away. It's wrong, Bill thinks, watching. Running away is a bad thing you get scolded for, even hit on the nose with newspaper. He watches other dogs scuttle out, the woman still chasing her hat.

Bill chooses and runs. He digs his hindquarters and races for the gate, banging a Weimaraner on the way—and then he's out, racing to catch the shepherd. It's easy to do, the shepherd hobbled. But he is now loping in a steady, altered three-legged canter, clear of purpose. Bill reaches him. The message from the shepherd has to do with distance, the need to leave the shelter behind. Back there, Bill hears shouting, faint in the wind. Ahead, a fallen palm frond whisks across the road. In seconds they reach the highway. They run west, side by side on the shoulder.

—Just run, the shepherd signals. —Don't look back. Run.

They do, together. Bill paces himself to match the slower dog. Everything now is wind. Everywhere leaves and torn seeds fly at them—they're running directly into the first hours of a storm that has brewed for days in the Caribbean. Now rain falls in sheets. It doesn't start small, there's no light pattering first, no slow build. It's thrown, pitched and dumped on all beneath. On the right the hot asphalt steams. Traffic barrels past, lashing the two dogs with waves. Horns bray. Headlights and fog lamps seem to charge all at once through the curtain, whipping past.

How far? A mile? All there is to know lives in his big legs and chest, energy and instinct. And the shepherd. Would Bill have run without him? Either way he has made another choice on another road, this one in Florida, in hurricane season, dodging a branch torn from a cabbage palm.

And in the clatter and steam of it, the slashing spray of passing cars—something registers. *I know this place.* In his brain, narrow but deep in terms of sound and smell, he is certain. Ahead, lights are flashing. Some cars have pulled off the road. Nearing them, Bill leads the shepherd, picking up more clearly the scent and certainty that he is right.

—This is good, he barks. —On the other side. I know what this is.

No time or need to think. He cuts right and dashes over asphalt. This is where he lives, this is the mister and missus, the pool and rugs, the bed to be under in storms like this. Tires skid, a horn blows. Still it blares. On the wide median he stops. The shepherd isn't with him. Bill looks back. He whines and barks, a surprise even to those hard pressed to get where they need to be in such a storm. For a moment, distracted from worry about their cars and houses they point at him, and at the shepherd struck in crossing, now crowded against the median's eastbound curb. Slowing, they inch along the right lane as others still race in the left, in the lane the shepherd did not manage to cross, many talking on cell phones, telling one more detail from this squall-soaked day on Davis Boulevard, telling the person on the other end about some crazy big dog out on the median, barking his damn head off in all this weather.

August is the cruellest month

If this afternoon the mister—the real one—were traveling in one of the passing cars, deafened by drumming on roof and hood and, slowed by the storm so that he all at once saw what was there, on the median, it would break his heart. He would divine much of what led to the moment, not the details, but the fundamentals. He would stop in the road. With furious drivers honking and yelling inside their own stopped cars, he would get out in the storm and call his dog. The other animal he would know was lost, hit hard by someone barreling down the fast left lane. And if anyone with him objected from inside his own car, concerned about upholstery or clothes, if anyone voiced objection to stopping under such conditions, he would probably have told that person to shut up. Or, he would say nothing, doing what must be done, acting on an imperative made absolute by the knowledge that what he was witnessing began with himself.

But he isn't there. He's playing golf on a public course outside Cadillac, Michigan.

Bouncing over the gravel secondary road to the Vinyls' lakefront place on this particular afternoon, a visitor is sure to know he has picked a perfect day to come. Unlike storm-tossed Naples, it's warm and dry, the road a shady tunnel splashed with sunny patches. Shifting with the breeze, the patches serve to animate the journey's static mood of enclosure and peace.

Pulling in and stopping outside the Vinyls' shiny corrugated pole barn (the landmark to look for from the road), the visitor walks along a cement path. Like the road, his passage here is canopied by maple and oak trees. He lets himself in at the gate (this and the fence added because of Bill), then walks to the back door of the big log house. The rarely used doorbell will sound tinny inside, like a bell in a warehouse.

But if the visitor knows better, he will instead follow the paver path to the right, bordered with impatiens. It ends at a broad bluestone patio laid before steps leading up to a screened porch. Both porch and patio run the length of the house. Down from this point, a grassy plain slopes for a hundred feet, ending at a narrow sand beach. The aluminum dock extends from this, and forty feet offshore floats a diving platform.

Today, the visitor will find Vinyl's wife knitting on the porch with Ruby and Ronald. This is after swims, and a trip to town, and puzzles on the floor after lunch. The missus hasn't knitted for twenty years, but her grandchildren now attend what in an earlier time was called a progressive school. This one is politically correct, with a curriculum that makes much of Native Americans, the environment, and healthy food. It also does everything possible to insure the children's studies are gender-neutral. Consequently, Ruby and Ronald are both knitting.

"You two are so quiet," the missus says.

"We're concentrating."

"Look—" Ronald holds his work up again, wanting approval every five minutes. His creation, not yet defined, is being made of electric blue chenille yarn.

"Beautiful. I'm very impressed."

He goes back to work. Over her own needles, the missus

watches his sister. If not yet a skillful knitter, Ruby is very fast. She is making another scarf, this one a not very appealing brown. In the last ten days she has made scarves for her father and grandparents, another for her mother, and one for her best friend back home in Brooklyn Heights. Isn't it time you made one for Jane? the missus asked on Sunday. I think that would be very nice. Ruby does what's expected of her, so that's what she has underway, a scarf for her stepmother. In her speed, the girl is dropping stitches, pulling her work apart and rushing on, driven it seems. For hours she keeps her long legs folded under her on the glider, getting up only when one of her feet falls asleep. Her eyes peer through the thick curtain of her hair. She frowns and purses her lips over the clicking needles.

An outboard motor whirs louder on the lake. Recognizable by pitch and speed as belonging to the boat of a neighbor, the missus glances out at it, then back to her granddaughter. She thinks Ruby's careless approach to the scarf might relate to her reading at school. She told them last night at dinner how her class of fourth graders has read both Lamb's Tales from Shakespeare, and simplified versions of the Homeric epics. She denounced Richard the Third ("He pays people to drown his own cousin in this barrel of wine. Then he kills his nephews"), sympathized with Romeo and Juliet ("really bad parents"), and judged Brutus to be a good but flawed man ("Ends don't justify the means").

Then she described the insults to Achilles' pride that explained his "wanting to be left alone." She went into detail about Telemachus and his efforts to learn about his long-missing father Odysseus. By then, everyone at the table had stopped eating. Her grandfather's trapped look made his missus feel for him. He was having to stand proxy on *this* coded message for his absentee son.

But Ruby had saved her greatest passion for Penelope. Over dessert, she went into careful detail about Odysseus' wife, beset by suitors demanding she choose one of them. It was painful, all of them held hostage at the kitchen table like so many Penelopes, under the glare of the Tiffany-style lamp. Holding her new baby, Ruby's stepmother could hardly miss knowing who the besieged wife really was. Ruby heaped praise on the long-suffering Penelope, providing details not offered by Homer. "She's in this big house," Ruby said. "All she wants is her husband. Everything was going great before he left. Now all these bogus people are forcing her to choose. She promises she'll do it right after she makes this sheet you put over dead people. A winding sheet. She's making one for Odysseus' father. The suitors can't say *anything* against her. Making this sheet's a custom. It's her duty, but every night she pulls it apart. That way, she'll never finish." Coming out of her trance, Ruby had taken up her fork. "But they figure it out," she said. "A maid tells one of the suitors."

A nice lake breeze now puffs the screen next to the missus. Yes, she thinks, knitting. Penelope gave Ruby her strategy. After the meal, brother and sister had gone down to skip stones off the dock. Still at the table, the new daughter-in-law smiled gamely. My pretty, gangly ten-year-old stepdaughter, she said. She's a supporter of male patriarchy. Holding the baby, she continued eating her pie.

A lawyer, the stepmother is taking a full year of maternity leave. That decision tipped the scales in her favor with the missus. So many now give birth, then six or eight weeks later hand over their new babies to caretakers, and go back to work. It's a version of "having it all" she does not approve of. But her son's second wife takes obvious pleasure in motherhood, and this has won over her mother-in-law. Holding the baby on her hip, she had used her napkin. Excellent pie, she said. It seems you have at least two Penelopes under your roof. What would be the equivalent of a golf widow in Ithaca? Sailing widow? Warrior widow? Ruby's situation is worse. All the suitors want her to like them.

She had left the table. Looking at her husband, the missus

waited until the rocker started on the porch. The mister was sipping another rob roy with his pie. You're having more of those lately, she told him. Am I? How many more? I'm not criticizing, she said. I just noticed. Do you have any suggestions? He shook his head. This is not good, Fred. Again he shook his head. That woman's got everything except Ruby, he said finally. Ronald's on board, not Ruby. Not because there's anything wrong with her stepmom. It's just not there yet. Maybe it won't ever be. No stepmom would be acceptable to Ruby, the missus told him. She wants her dad's undivided attention.

Her husband had folded deeply suntanned forearms on the table. I don't know, honey, he said. I can take them fishing, I can work another hundred jigsaw puzzles. I don't have a thing to offer on this.

The storm lasts all day and all night. By mid-morning, the last of it has come ashore, moved inland and blown itself out.

A stunned quiet settles over Donegal Golf and Country Club. It blankets streets littered with palm fronds, the silence broken only by the gurgle of overburdened sewers. People cautiously part drapes and draw back vertical blinds. They see battered flowerbeds, wave-like patterns of mulch dislodged from their landscaping, swimming pools overflowing their decks.

By two o'clock, the off-again, on-again sound of chain saws is breaking the silence. Nail guns and hammers join in, popping and knocking as crews set about repairing the damage. It isn't severe—nothing like Wilma the year before. The power never went out. But heavy palm fronds have dropped through quite a few pool cages. Roof tiles will need replacing on the clubhouse and golf-cart shed. Casual water will figure for days on all but five of the fairways, and a small assessment will be needed to replace surveillance cameras torn from posts.

In fact, while glad nothing too serious has come of the storm, those with more serious damage regret that the highest recorded wind speed fell shy of tropical-storm status. Without that designation, no name was given, and a no-name storm means insurance policies will pay nothing.

People come out to pick up and rake their yards. Skimming

pools, they call to each other and trade stories. They laugh in an unspoken understanding that those who stay through the summer have something on Donegal owners who go north and are fooling around in dull places like Michigan and Illinois.

Because of so much activity, no one passes along the brick path behind the Vinyls' pool cage.
The frame is intact. The overhead screen sags a bit from leaves and a dead mourning dove. The heavy stone and glass patio table, always left outside, trembles with water. The house itself has sustained no damage. Secure behind hurricane shutters, after eight weeks it is as close and lightless as a tomb.
But even if someone were to pass the Vinyls' place this afternoon, he might not see the dog there, under the table. And if in the days following someone happens to note a break in the screen door, that will be unremarkable, given the storm. Perhaps the passerby might make a mental note, but not feel a need to enter the cage and check on things.
Stunned, the big dog stays where he is all morning. He is unconvinced it's over.

From the first certainty on the road that he knew where he was, Bill didn't need to think. When the shepherd didn't respond or move in the gutter, horns honking, Bill spun away and bounded across Davis. Pounding up the entrance drive, then under the barrier gate (the guard long gone from his post), he sought shelter there first. When lightning touched down on his right, he ran howling to the club's restaurant entrance. It was where the mister had come for beer and talk, Bill waiting on the lawn outside. At some point the memory led to a sense of urgency about going to the house. The mister had left him and gone on alone, something had happened to him.
Seeking shelter, the dog worked his way next to the ficus hedge that marked the outer perimeter of the property. No other

protection would figure between this point and the street of houses. The ficus, too dense to push through, meant he must run exposed on his left. A lightning strike touched down ahead, visible on the course. Bill barked in fear, still running, raking the hedge. Then came the lightning's mortar-shell explosion, thunder so big it shook the ground. The dog cowered against the hedge. Then continued. Twice, vehicle headlights raked past, first those of the greens keeper's pickup, then a security SUV.

In this way the dog reached the house. It was at the height of the storm when he shoved at the screen door in the old way. Lightning strikes were coming now almost continuously, neon veins out on the course followed by artillery rounds. He bumped through the door. At the place where the doorwall should be, standing on hind legs and taller than some men, he pawed the steel shutter. Metal slats thundered under his paws, the dog lost to fear, whimpering and confused. Confined to what he knew, Bill had found his home. That meant the mister was here, too. Inside, with the missus. If his dog beat long enough, kept barking and pawing on what was over the doorwall, he would come. Small metal spurs on the shutter slats broke the soft skin between the pads of the dog's paws. No matter. It would open, soon the mister would shove apart the glass and Bill would scuttle under the bed. The mister would not leave this time but stay there in the room telling him It's all right, old sport, it's all right, cool your jets—

* * * *

But he didn't come. Barking, crying after the fashion of big dogs in a state of fear—not a high sound but guttural, alarming—the animal at last squeezed his body flush with the house wall. The table offered some shelter, left under the covered part of the lanai.

But the storm. The eleventh fairway lay flat and vulnerable. Even those neighbors still in their houses, those who dared peek through their drapes would later insist that, name or no name, something big had gone on out there. It was weather so powerful, one said, it seemed to have a personality. An identity. And they would all insist that this presence had concentrated itself right outside, down on the eleventh fairway.

The sound of repairs continues after dark. The dog stays huddled. Confused by the chain saws, he knows they are not part of the storm, but is still so frightened he waits for them to stop.

They do, just before midnight. He stays where he is a while longer, then unfolds himself. Tentatively, he steps out from the wall, onto the deck. By this time, the overflowing swimming pool has returned to near-normal level. He hears a television. He steps to the pool's edge and drinks noisily. It tastes better than usual, the concentration of chemicals diluted by eight inches of rain. When done, he turns and looks again at the shuttered doorwall. Having eaten nothing all day, he whimpers, wanting in, wanting his bowls and the food the mister gives him, made with chicken broth. The idea makes him hungrier. He thinks to again paw the shutter, but moves instead to the screen door. He pushes. As with herding Ronald, when he understands it won't open out, Bill shoves and claws the screen. The stuff gives, stretches. His untrimmed nails rake the nylon, the left paw shoving through as it did ten weeks ago. He pushes his head through, his big shoulders. Clear, the dog roams the familiar beds, beaten flat.

But the weeks away have changed him. He is wary, cautious. Even in the dark, he stays near the house, out of sight. He has a fear of strangers, of those who drag you to trucks and cages, who catch you after being in the shelter yard and put you back inside. People who take you some strange place with a yard, throwing balls but then giving you up. In some true sense, experience has stolen Bill's innocence.

But he is starving. His big appetite and workhorse metabolism demand food. When all sounds of machinery and TV have stopped, he ventures farther afield, into other yards. He polices the perimeter of what had been his territory, sniffing, rooting. The nature of life in a tropical climate dictates that people take special care with garbage. Anything organic becomes a magnet for ants and vermin, so residents bag everything twice and keep their trash barrels inside the garage.

He finds nothing. Most of the yards have been cleared, the street as well. Water still stands in pools on lawns. He returns to the back of the mister's cage and looks out. The sky has cleared. It isn't hot, and the moon now reveals the fairway. Monitoring the air for any scent of food, Bill smells life. It comes from the jungle rough opposite. Less pronounced because of the heavy rainfall, the smell of swamp also stinks of chemicals. Low to the ground, he begins slowly working down the incline. When he reaches the course, the big dog lopes over the fairway, smelling something animal. It's there to him, not in doubt, and now come other smells. His big paws sink in swales formed overnight in the sod. The sound he makes is that of a horse cantering in beach surf.

When he comes to the point Ronald had reached before being stopped, the dog slows. He walks now, nearing the bone-white trunks of melaleuca trees. If he does not remember Hotspur telling him in Dog about Randy the golden retriever, and alligators, he remembers something. A caution. Some admonition weeks before that led him to tear through screening and herd a child as he had seen the border collie do with golfers.

So, although starving, he hesitates before entering the undergrowth. It's mostly saw palmetto, very dense. He gives all his famished self to receiving what the senses of smell and sound bring to him. Something dead. Chemicals. The discreet *point* sound of single water drops falling from trees into standing pools. Cabbage palms, a few live oaks that have seeded themselves. Bamboo, toads, a type of snail that doesn't crack even when clamped in a big dog's jaw. His new fear of humans gives way to necessity. He prowls outside the wall of undergrowth, and finds a way in. He begins searching.

If Bill actually remembered talk of alligators, of game wardens bringing poles fitted with loops like those used on rottweilers, it might be better for him. He might then overcome his present fear of men and go looking for anyone at all—a security guard, a service worker on night duty buffing floors or changing high hat lights in the clubhouse, jobs best done when people are asleep.

Not better because a large gator is there, hungry itself and motionless, waiting to break legs with its tail, then drag its prey under water. In fact, Emma's version—her mistress's—that Randy lost his leg to a lawn mower is closer to the truth. Not a mower but a hedge trimmer had severed the golden's leg—not here, but on the opposite side of the undeveloped property. Calling out in the most awful of dog cries, those reserved for mortal wounds, Randy had made it through the rough, to be found on the eleventh by a passing foursome playing their round before lunch.

But it might have been better, because Bill would not then find the drowned king snake. Kings are big, and he tears and shakes it, holding it down with his paws, pulling. Need gives him strength and he works at it, a task uncommon for a dog accustomed to bowls and Science Diet. But instinct and hunger keep him going, grinding bones, devouring inner organs, even the half-digested litter of baby mice in the snake's stomach. It's not good, not right, but food.

When he can eat no more, the dog finds his way back to the break in the dense saw palmetto. He emerges before the plain of grass glistening with moonlight. Driven into hiding by the storm, insects are now reclaiming the night. They fill the heavy air with sound. Following his own prints, he recrosses the fairway, then trots up the incline. The dog does not look elsewhere, or again prowl the outer edges of his territory. He goes back and opens the door in the old way, pushing on the frame. That it still works as before—nose first, then the pneumatic door sliding along his flank—fits with the dog's wish to recover his life, the right master, days as they should be.

Reflexes slowed, he yelps at the pinch on his tail. Bill draws the rest of him inside. Still, even the pinched tail adds to Bill's confidence. He walks back to the place under the table. Settling flat against the wall, he faces out.

Five minutes? Ten? At last he settles his muzzle between paws smelling of snake. No longer starving, Bill remains alert. His sense of return, of having recovered the place where he belongs—is real enough. Insects throb in the darkness. The enclosure and table, four heavy ceramic planters left out, his territory and the world beyond the cage all register. But they cannot displace the jangled mix of memories since Vinyl. This is where he should be. Where, then, is the mister and missus? They go places sometimes, leaving him alone—"Hold down the fort, Bill"—but always he is left inside the quiet house with its cool tile floors. Never like this. And he is fed first. After, he watches at the front window for the silver van. It comes back. Always.

The Donegal golf course remains closed for a week. It hardly matters to most residents. The return of sultry heat and humidity make play impossible, at least for the most senior members. Outsiders who come to play at cheap summer rates are turned away. Until they dry out, there is no point in damaging the course's tees and greens.

The residents stay indoors for several days. They don't think about it, but the storm has shaken them. They half believe it might come back. No one takes a nightly constitution along the back path. They walk their dogs to the nearest corner and back, trowel and plastic baggy in hand. Or, they let them out to take care of business. Although forbidden by club rules, this latter approach has been adopted by Luger's mister. And Chiffon's mistress never risks her stylist's handiwork by going anywhere in such humid weather. The two dogs meet behind Trust Fund's house, sniff, and mark. As the bichon squats, fuchsia ribbon quivering, the schnauzer lifts his leg with assertive gusto. Were she there, Madame might call out "Sieg heil!"

Now they stand in back of Glenda Gilmore's cage. Music is playing. The dark lanai dances in an eery blue haze rising from the pool's subsurface lights. Floating on an air mattress, Glenda is humming to the music.

—No one is outside in this heat, Luger says in clipped Dog dialect. —People stay inside the house.

—She must like it, Chiffon says. —She floats on something. Drinking something.

—She sings, Luger says. —What is this singing? It hurts dogs' ears.

—She likes it. She cries. She floats. It makes me sad. I cried, too. She saw me and said hello, Chiffon. Then she sang. I heard her say *Hotsie*.

They watch a while longer. What Chiffon heard earlier was Glenda performing karaoke for an audience of one. But she is no longer actually singing. She's just floating, humming as she listens to Nat King Cole, drinking gin and tonics until she can face food. She's not through mourning, but the collie's death shifted the process to a new phase. Now, Glenda swims, does yoga. She exercises with dumbbells until she can't raise the weights. She has come to believe physical exhaustion will eventually drain and squeeze away the blues. But these exertions are also a form of self-punishment. The dog's death has come to represent a betrayal of trust, a product of neglect that somehow confirms the bad opinion of her held by so many at Donegal. She married Cliff Gilmore for his vitality, not his money. All right, for his money, too, but that was a bonus. And because he made her laugh. After the dog's death, nothing seems to matter.

—Nobody does this, Luger says. Maybe she's dead.

—She moves. See?

—She should do something. I don't like it. Why float like that? My mister plays, reads. He watches. Uses the computer thing. I have to bark to be fed.

—A man comes to the house— Just then, a high note being held by Nat Cole makes Chiffon's ears move. She waits. —He helps my missus do things. He says something over and over, she touches her feet. When he doesn't come, she touches her feet watching him on the TV.

Luger shakes his head free of noseeums. In August, they are very thick. —Live and work, he says. —Then die. She should be doing.

Both of them now hear the sound of a dog being sick. Glenda doesn't hear it, still floating. The sound comes again. Together, the two turn away and trot along the brick path. Again the noise comes. They pass three empty houses, the patio tables draped in tarps. Overhead, screens sag with leaves no one is home to blow off. Reaching the Vinyl house, they see nothing, but hear it again. Chiffon follows Luger along the cage.

—Bill, he says, smelling the scent. —Bill! Silence. The schnauzer reaches the door and sticks his head through the rent in the screen. Knowing who it has to be but also smelling sickness, he steps in gingerly. Chiffon is afraid and whimpers. —Bill?

At first, the dog can't get up. Three of the four days spent here have been followed by nightly trips to the jungle rough. He has eaten more snake, found a dead bird. But the rough's acreage, abandoned as unprofitable by the developer, has since become a refuse dump for work crews tending the course. It's less trouble to empty the last dregs of mulch here, the rotten railroad ties used to shore up cart paths, dead plants, fertilizers. And pesticides. The latter, a mix of Round Up and Preen used to kill weeds growing in flower beds and paver joints, has leached into the rough's swampy water. Even the storm's eight-inch rainfall didn't break down its chemical strength. Pounding at the steel shutter the first night, the dog cut his paws. The cuts were made worse by tearing through the screen door. Through the cuts, the pesticides have entered his system.

He struggles up to meet the schnauzer. He makes no move to greet the other dog, docile and shaky as Luger noses him. —What's wrong with you? You smell wrong.

—I don't know.

—Why are you shaking?

He sees the bichon outside, but has no strength. It tires him to stand.

—Many things happened, Luger says. —Emma left. They took her missus somewhere. Emma went with the ones who visit.

—They came with a truck, Chiffon calls. —My mistress was walking me. They carried what you sit on.

—*Furniture*, Luger tells her, not turning. —Did you run away?

—Yes. The shaking makes Bill feel unstable. Slowly he refolds himself on the deck. He is panting, not from heat, from poison. —I ran, he says.

—That's wrong. Never run.

—Tell about the dachshunds, Chiffon calls.

The poison is making Bill dizzy. He works again to stand.

—Tell about the dachshunds, Chiffon says again.

—They didn't leave. Something happened. Stanzi says the other den is gone. Her missus cries like Glenda, but the mister didn't die. She yells, Stanzi says. He doesn't talk. We can see them.

He wants to move, and manages to stand. The dizziness and vomiting have made him think he will never get up if he lies down again. He pads across the deck. Passage in and out has widened the hole. He steps through, Luger behind. He lets the other dogs lead. Seeing Bill's outline trailing after would surprise anyone who knows the dogs in this part of Donegal. Still tall, he is now gaunt. His backbone forms a ridge, ribs visible. The process of decline began last month and has speeded up with the poison. He understands something in the jungle rough caused it, because of the sensation in his paws. He stopped going, but the sickness is worse.

One house, two. Twice the two dogs come back when he stops. Something is wrong, and they exercise a kind of deference, not because of Bill's size but in response to the smell of sickness. They go on. When they pass the Yorkies' lanai, Chiffon says, —They left. Before Emma.

—They always go, Luger says. —They come and go. My master calls them *snowbirds*.

By the time they reach the Telecoms' cage, all three dogs are panting. They find Wolfi and Stanzi lying outside the doorwall. The light is on inside, the drapes drawn. When he sees them, Wolfi gets up and begins his duck walk waddle along the screen. Panting, Stanzi remains before the entrance. Her chestnut coat has a glossy sheen in the amber light passing through the drapes.

—It's bad, Wolfi says, coming. —What can we do? We're small dogs, they forget now. They leave us out, they close the door. We bark, they don't come. It's bad.

Still communicating in his own nervous way, the dachshund reaches them. Wolfi gives no sign of knowing Bill's been gone. —We have to stay here now, he says. —All the time, in this heat. We're not made for it, it's no good. No airplane, no bag under the seat. The mister has no boat, we never go fishing. He won't play golf. I miss the car, we just stay here every day. The missus throws things. It's dangerous. Even before the storm, we stay under the bed.

* * * *

"Jesus Christ, you scared me!"

He doesn't get up for her. He can't. The following morning he is back under the table. The pool girl bends to see him. "Bill! What're you doing there?" She watches him panting, smells him. "Where's your people?" Vomit and feces mark the deck. "Aw, what'd you get into? Remember me? Brianna?"

The dog always greeted her, wanting to play. If the owner didn't hold him, he jumped in the pool when she started working, whining when he was pulled out as she added chemicals. Seeing his labored breathing, the way his bony ribs are pumping, she thinks he must be drinking from it. Brianna decides to hold off putting in the chlorine and bleach. She stands and finishes scrubbing the pool's side tiles, looking over and talking in a soft voice he recognizes.

An hour later, rolling thunder announces the afternoon shower. They occur almost daily during the summer. Soon, it is raining. Bill doesn't care. Under the table, he pants without stopping, whimpering reflexively. The dog has withdrawn. Sometime before the shower ends, two men from Animal Recovery come around the front of the house. Soaked through and shielding his eyes, one of them points. "There he is. He's big. You never see a dog like that at a club."

"I know this one." The other man opens the door. His scent—the molecular history of shelter dogs, medicine, disinfectant—all of it crowds forward as he approaches the table. Bill rises up, the table banging his back, riding his spine. He growls, making the eating sound.

"Whoa." The man, stops. The dog is shaking. As soon as the man steps back, Bill folds himself and lies panting.

"Well, she said he was sick, but he's still in there punching. Go get the loop."

Ruby Thursday

In Lake City, the son comes at the end of July, for a whole week. Both kids swarm him, dodge and tackle, demand he stand them on their heads. It heartens their stepmother. He swims with them, throws them screaming off the diving platform. They fish. Grandpa drives the runabout while his son, never much good at it, wobbles, but finally rises on water skis. Dragged then in life vests behind the boat on inner tubes, Ruby and Ronald yell "Faster!"

He takes them to miniature golf, to a carnival with rides in Cadillac. Then it's time for him to go see to final details at the new house outside Philadelphia. Before he leaves, Ronald asks questions about his new school. The children's mother has readily agreed that it makes more sense for Ronald and Ruby to attend school in Pennsylvania. She called them regularly all month, asking chatty questions about other children at the lake, their knitting, was the antibiotic working on Ronald's ear infection, Bloomingdale's was having a pre-school sale on kids' parkas, would their stepmom please measure their chests and arm lengths. They would now be spending just weekends—every other—in Brooklyn Heights. It's mom's job, she explained. That, and being alone. Back and forth from Manhattan, it takes away all the time we have together. She wants their sympathy, but is actually looking forward to the new arrangement. When asked if the plan sounded all right to her, Ruby was watching *Shrek* on the set in her grandparents' bedroom, sprawled on a big bed made of logs. She shrugged and said "Whatever." It was perfectly clear to her that ten-year-olds were too young to vote, that all they wanted from her was passive agreement. She gave it, but nothing more.

Her father leaves in the morning. That evening, Ruby's stepmother comes out on the porch with the baby. She sits and rocks, looking out on the lake. By prearrangement, Ronald has gone to town with his grandparents. The chair creaks. Ruby is not knitting tonight. She is stringing beads, making necklaces and bracelets. She said no to going to town, but now realizes this never happens, being left alone with her stepmother.

"I lost something today, Ruby."

No, the two of them are never left this way. Why do it? They have nothing to say. She is always trying to get answers during meals. Or holds up magazines, asking, Would this color look good in your new room? What kind of bedspread is cool now? She has everything but Ruby, and will not get that. The girl strings more beads, wanting now to watch a video, one of the old favorites she is too old for but all at once wants to see. Winnie, or Elmo.

"Or maybe I didn't lose it," her stepmother says. "Do you know what it was?" Ruby keeps working. Sometimes, if you just don't answer, or say *I'm concentrating*, they leave you alone. "I think you do. I never take it off unless I go swimming. It's the cold water, it shrinks my fingers. Did you hide it or throw it in the lake?"

Ruby's heart is pounding. A good girl but lost, she wants a video from before. She feels frightened. Not of her stepmother, whom she knows in fact to be generous and attentive in ways her own mother is not. She doesn't even hate her. That's what her stepmother told dad two days before, in their bedroom, thinking the door was closed—She hates me.

"Either way, Ruby, you have to understand something—"

The chair rocks, the baby burps. Ruby strings beads without

looking over, afraid now. You aren't going to be punished, she thinks. Nothing ever works, nothing will change. "I love your father," her stepmother says. "I love you, I love your brother, I love your grandparents. I even *almost* love your mother, don't ask me why. I suppose because she's charming in an off-the-wall way. And I love your new baby brother—"

The rocker seems louder, supporting her stepmother, giving her strength. "I'm getting a new wedding band when we go back. If you take it, I'll get another. It won't matter, Ruby, I'm not going anywhere. However long it takes, you have to give me a chance."

A Good Act of Contrition

Air conditioning keeps the dogs comfortable. It also helps reduce odor, something important to making a good impression on those who come to look and, possibly, fill out the shelter's adoption questionnaire. There are two rows of cages. The one for smaller dogs runs two high, smallest on top, bigger ones below.

The second row holds large dogs. High-gloss green paint covers walls and crates, the same green on the floor. Skylights brighten the room during the morning. When they dim, the dogs begin to whine. All of them hate thunder. During electrical storms they bark and howl in a way that makes the more sensitive staff members feel helpless.

One of them keeps putting off the inevitable. Obviously, Bill won't survive. As with heartworm, the shelter vet has done blood work, deciding the cost of necessary medications argues against treatment. Bill's run is over, he said. Too bad. But the girl in charge this week keeps bringing water and food. He doesn't eat, but each time she looks in she feels a sense of guilt. It was she who chased a hat, talking on her cell phone to her boyfriend as half a dozen dogs ran from the pen. Three were recovered, one of them since adopted. They found the shepherd but not Bill, and a dalmatian mix.

* * * *

"He was adopted." The girl stops in front of the cage.

"What happened? He ran away?"

"The guy brought him back."

"Why?"

"He thought he'd be a good watch dog. Because of his size. He got robbed with Bill in the house. It was sort of funny, he did this routine with Bill showing the thief where everything was."

The woman kneels and looks in. "Oh no."

"Yeah. But it's nice of you to come see him." The girl attendant has a strong impulse to confess what happened. She thinks better of it. "He should've been put down by now."

The woman keeps looking in. If Bill recognizes her, he gives no sign. Skin and bones. His panting is awful to her. "He can't be saved?"

The girl knows it's wrong. The dog won't survive, but she doesn't want to euthanize him. No one will ever know what happened that day, but she knows. Like the Colonel and his drowned Yorkie, she does not want this dog put down on her watch.

"Well—" she kneels next to the woman. "The vet says there is a treatment. His ears are infected. I think he also has parasites." Yes, it's wrong, but she adds, "You can never be sure, though."

Glenda fills out the form. Staff members in the office look at each other. They shrug and raise eyebrows. People who adopt dogs have a great many different agendas. She starts to write the nominal check, but stops. "Could I see your vet? Could I pay for him to talk to me?"

The vet has them bring Bill in. He shows her how to put the capsules in his mouth. The dog swallows as the vet holds his muzzle and strokes his neck. Then he uses the eardrops. Even dying, the dog pulls away. "This is always hard," he says. "Sick or not, they hate it." A second medicine to be put in water and food will treat parasites. A third may or may not counteract the chemical poisoning.

She pays for them to bring him in a crate. She leads them west on Davis in her car. At the Donegal gatehouse, she explains that the van behind her is making a delivery. The gate rises. They take the route she has described, passing along a broad boulevard. The two shelter workers comment on the course's beauty, the sweeping fairways that dip and angle in doglegs.

At the house, they open the van and carry the crate between them, waiting as she unlocks the door. Inside, the two men stop in the foyer. "Where to?"

It seems to confuse her. "I don't know. Where do you think?"

"Your dog, ma'am."

"Please take him up there—"

They carry the crate through the house, past unkempt rooms. At the back they stop, looking at each other over the cage. The big room's furniture has been pushed against the walls. Squared on the rug lies a woven mat marked with the stark, black and white symbol for yin and yang. Surrounding the mat, incense burners and joss sticks in slender holders rest next to empty glasses and bottles.

"Here?"

"Facing out, so he can see."

They lower it. She tips and thanks them, sees them to the door, thanks them again. When they're gone, she comes back and kneels. She opens the crate door to see better. She goes in the kitchen, returning with a stainless steel dish of water. She gets down again and places it before the dog.

It confuses him. Having given up, resembling shelter dogs that can never adjust to life with humans and will therefore never be adopted, Bill stares at the bowl without seeing. For the first time in three days, he thinks of something. A small, shiny brown thing, a dog lies panting outside a closed doorwall. It's night, there are bugs. Light glistens on the dog's back, a dachshund's. She is looking at him with defeat, unwilling to get up and join the other dachshund walking to him, complaining in Dog about something.

His last impression before being taken away. But the confusion comes from something else. Senses diminished, he still smells whatever it is. He knows it and the dog it belongs to. The smell comes from the bowl of water. Now, from the air outside the cage, more of Hotspur meets his nostrils. Bill can't move, but knows Hotspur lives here, with the woman on all fours looking at him.

* * * *

The thought of giving the pills scares her. Every time she gets down to look at him, his head seems bigger, the jaws intimidating. When it comes time for the first pill, she gets down again. "Come on, Bill, please—"

He won't leave the crate. Frustrated after fifteen minutes of pleading, Glenda removes the water dish. She gets behind the cage and raises it. The dog half tumbles, half crawls out. Still partially inside when she comes around to him, he won't look at her. Trembling, she kneels again and holds her hand in front of his nose. He seems not to notice. To give herself courage, she goes out to the garage and comes back tugging on a golf glove.

She reviews what the vet showed her. Force open the mouth by squeezing, gently but firmly on both sides. Quickly toss in the pill and try to hold the muzzle closed. Sometimes it won't work and he'll spit it out, the vet said. If not, smooth the throat this way. On her first try, nerves get the better of her. She manages to get the mouth open, but fails with the pill. "Damn!" She picks it up, waits for her breathing to regulate, and tries again. With a healthy Bill, the process would be impossible for her. But Bill's weakness and resignation work in her favor. She succeeds on the third try.

It elates her. She feels a sense of accomplishment. No, she feels triumph, hope. It's why you got him, she thinks. Learning from the pool girl about the dog found outside a house closed for the season, she had known which it was. Hotsie liked him, she told the girl. They got along.

That's what they're for, she thinks smoothing the dog's throat. That's what they do for you, Cliff said. They free you in a way. You can do this, Glenda tells herself. Still she smooths the dog's throat, holding his heavy lower jaw. At least you can try.

But it doesn't look good. At five, she leaves and comes back with half a dozen kinds of dog food. Two are brands Hotspur liked, the other four recommended by the manager at Pet Warehouse. She goes to the kitchen, opens cans and bags and spoons or dumps all six in separate soup bowls. The bowls belong to the set of china given to her as a wedding gift by the director of the modeling agency she worked for. She puts the bowls in front of the open cage—Bill has gone back in. "Come on, do it for me. This matters. We're doing the pills whether you like it or not. We're doing the ears and worm stuff. We have to get tough, we have to get it together. Please help me."

She sits with him all evening, talking this way. Several times she leaves and comes back with chew toys and balls of Hotspur's. She's decided that the more such objects near him, the better. She greatly exaggerates the meaning of the dogs' friendship. She convinces herself it will work the way close attachments sometimes bring about miracles on *Animal Planet*. She and Cliff watched the sentimental stories of rescues, crimes foiled by family pets. She would not admit it, but Glenda thinks in terms of Hotspur's soul having returned, having reentered the house to keep vigil with her in a friend's hour of need. Oddly, she has no confidence in the notion of human souls, but would not see a contradiction.

There is none, really. Dog and master are joined in her mind. She wants to believe, be redeemed, she wants to turn her own corner.

Glenda makes up her mind about something. She stands and walks quickly down the hall. Turning into one of two spare bedrooms, almost immediately she steps out lugging a small TV. The cord trails after. "I don't know what works. Who knows what works? I'm not telling and don't you, either. This is an emergency, in emergencies what's wrong with trying anything at all?"

She balances the TV against her hip, resting it on a chair before reaching down to move food bowls. She picks up the television and lowers it to the floor in front of the crate. Satisfied, Glenda runs the cord to a wall socket and plugs it in. A grainy picture forms, a Seinfeld rerun. She steps to the big TV stand in front of her yoga mat, picks up a tape, returns and inserts it in the small set before sitting on the floor next to Bill.

"That's at Naples beach. In January. We had that great two-week stretch. Just about perfect, low humidity. Then it got cold, but those two weeks. That's me, Cliff had the camera. Oh watch this… Isn't that amazing? You couldn't fool Hotsie. You could try but you would never succeed. All right, this is funny—" Glenda laughs. "Right in there with college kids on spring break, stealing the ball. See there? Herding them."

Does any of it mean a thing to a poisoned Lab mix in a strange house? Probably not. But the smells here all make a kind of sense to him. Food, the collie. And if he doesn't recognize Hotspur on the screen, he sees a dog. Muzzle between his paws, when a bark issues from the soundtrack, Bill corrects his ears.

She brings her air mattress in from the lanai and stretches out on the floor. Pleading with him to eat, she heats up a chicken pot pie for herself. She eats in front of him, to set an example. If he wants human food, he'll have it. Leftover steak, a slice of pizza she warms up in the microwave. She tries to remember what treats the collie liked. Hot dogs. She gets some from the freezer and needlessly boils them. Peanut butter. She spoons a dollop onto a cheese board.

Later, with a different home video playing, she does her yoga. But she burns no incense. Hotspur hadn't liked it. When she is done, Glenda turns off all but the lamp in the foyer and stretches out on the air mattress. Looking at the motionless dog, she feels sleepy.

When she wakes, early morning light fills the doorwall. She looks at the dog. In the night he has shifted to face away. She thinks he's dead, then sees shallow breathing. Too rapidly, the dog's rib rack is pumping. But Bill has made it through the night. And is she making it up? Looking down at what now strikes her as an embarrassing, ridiculous banquet spread out on the tile floor, she chooses to believe some of the sliced hunks of hot dog are missing. When she touches him, the dog raises his head, sighs and lowers it. When she repeats the cage-lifting, he comes all the way out before settling. She puts in the morning pill and keeps talking, stroking his neck, his back. He tries to shake her away when she squeezes the lotion in his ears, but he doesn't snap. Real or imagined, every small success strengthens her. She keeps trying to get him to look at her. She smells funky to herself, but is reluctant to shower. That he held on until morning has raised the ante, made her nervous, afraid to leave him. From time to time aware again of the buffet, Glenda wonders if perhaps she is having a breakdown.

"No, I'm not. I'm just giving it the old college try. And you will too, won't you?" When she sits next to him and gets ready to give him the midday pill, she isn't wearing the golf glove. Stroking his neck, she faces the bright doorwall. The steamy day hovers outside, grass and trees a deep green true only in summer. For the first time since waking Glenda realizes she slept through the night. "That doesn't happen now. Almost never. It's because of alcohol. It puts you to sleep, but it wakes you up." She mixed no drinks last night.

She isn't wrong about hot dogs. Bill likes them. Hot dogs or brats are something the mister grilled for himself when others wanted chicken. He always made one or two for the dog. And Bill drinks some water, the bowl smelling familiar, trustworthy. The woman's voice appeals to him. He lies outside the cage, watching her in the kitchen. Then she does something sitting on the floor, in front of the big TV.

He sleeps, she makes him take the pills, fools with his ears. Whenever he wakes she is in the room. On the third day, he stands. She claps her hands, holds his head in both hands like the mister, and goes on talking. She opens the doorwall and coaxes him to come out. Like a true convalescent, he pads to the opening and looks out warily. It isn't right, too full of scents and challenges he has no strength for. He turns away and goes back inside the crate.

She calls the vet, asking if this means Bill will live. "Dogs rally like people," he says. "I'm surprised he got this far, but don't get your hopes too high." Pointless advice. Glenda is by now convinced. Possessed. Rally and then fail? Out of the question. She redoubles her efforts, goes back for more pills and a dietary supplement the vet suggests. She commits herself utterly to the dog, fully freed now of self-doubt or questions. She has become a fanatic, a zealot. Even before Cliff Gilmore's death, she never believed in God. What, then, are you praying to? she asks herself that afternoon, under the shower and hearing herself doing just that, voice hollow in the tiled stall.

I'm Nobody, Are you Nobody too?

The one-on-one conversation on the porch does not lead to what Ruby's stepmother calls *rapprochement*. After the talk Ruby is, if anything, even more unhappy. When Fred asks if she wants to make another visit with Ronald to the traveling carnival in Cadillac, she says no thank you. She keeps knitting and doing beadwork, isolating herself. She prefers her old friend the Game Boy to TV with others. After dinner, she still lets her grandfather sit her on his lap and work the wheel of the big pontoon boat. But it isn't the same. Later, he sees her staring out at the dock.

Two days before the three of them are to go back to the temporary house being rented in Pennsylvania, his new daughter-in-law comes up from her afternoon swim. "Could we talk?" She is toweling her hair. They walk down the greensward to the Adirondack chairs. Seated with the towel draped around her shoulders, she sits back. "You know I'm in for the long haul," she says. Fred does know that, it's obvious. His son's second wife is no short-ball hitter. "I have a BA from a good school and a law degree from a better one. Big deal. I need a few days to regroup and imagine how we're going to manage this fall. Ruby just isn't letting me in. I'd like her to stay with you for ten more days while we sort things out. She loves you both so much. It would mean a lot."

He always flies down in late August to check on the Naples house. As usual, there have been storms and he worries about damage to the appliances. Lightning strikes can fry the wiring and turn complicated circuits into blobs of plastic and silicon. "Why not take Ruby?" his wife says. "Would you like that, sweetheart, just the two of you? Take the plane with grandpa?"

Maybe she is just bored, or perhaps her experiences in Florida have resonated in some way. She nods yes. The following night, they take the 6:20 Spirit flight, arriving at the Fort Myers airport at nine. They take the limo to Donegal, and then Ruby helps roll up the hurricane shutters. Everything in the close, sealed house has survived. The air conditioning is left on to prevent mold, but the rooms are musty. Reset at a lower temp, the system begins to clear the house. Ruby and Fred share a frozen pizza, then go to bed. In the morning, they are eating toaster waffles on the lanai when the pool girl comes.

"You had a dog," she says using the tile brush. "Bill?"

"That's right. We had to give him up."

"You took him to the shelter?"

"We thought maybe it was best."

"Can I go inside, grandpa?"

"Sure, sweetie."

As the doorwall slides shut, the pool girl reaches down with glass vials. She takes water samples and holds them up, checking the PH level. "I don't know what happened." She watches the vials change color. "He must've got out. He came back. He was right where you're sitting, under the table last week when I came. I called Animal Services. I was down doing the Gilmores', I told her about it."

* * * *

He goes inside and calls Glenda. He has never learned about Hotspur and she tells him. She explains about going to the shelter and bringing Bill home. "He's very sick, Fred. Please come, it might do him good."

"Do you want to see Bill?" He puts down the cordless phone. Ruby is on the sofa in the living room with the Game Boy. "Come on. Let's take a walk and see old Bill, what do you say?" Reluctantly, Ruby sets aside the toy. They leave by the front door and start up the block. "You liked him," her grandfather says. "You two always got along." She keeps silent. When he explained earlier in the summer to both grandchildren why he and grandma had decided it was best to give up Bill, Ruby had been knitting. Just because of the stupid baby, she said. He gets kicked out of his house. His wife tried to convince her someone would be sure to adopt a nice dog like Bill, but Ruby knew her grandmother had not much liked the dog. You don't *know* that, grandma, she said. You're just saying it.

The doorbell is still echoing inside when Glenda opens the door. "Fred—" She steps into his arms as is her way. It's a generational thing, all this hugging. Glenda's approach to greeting behavior has always made other Donegal wives furious. Unable to do anything about it, they are forced to watch their geezer husbands looking proud to be hugged so *thoroughly* by someone so much younger and thinner and the rest of it.

As the hug goes on, with Ruby waiting for what will soon follow, one of the standard token greetings for children—*And who's this?,* or *My, how you've grown*—the vigorously circulating air in the Gilmore house now carries information to all corners of the interior. It is information at the molecular level, most of which would not mean anything to humans.

The vet has said that sick dogs, like sick humans, sometimes rally, then decline rapidly. With Bill, it's too soon to tell. He is eating almost nothing. He drinks water, he fusses about the ear treatments, then lies flat again, panting. But when the information floating now over the receptors still at work in his nose join what is coming to his ears, he stops panting and raises his head. It confuses him but it is real. *That* voice, *that* scent. He struggles to undo his stick legs. His paws skitter and scratch, seeking purchase on slippery tile. He is shaking but up, looking to the foyer when the mister sees him.

"Oh no—"

Why doesn't he come? Here I am, Bill thinks. It's me.

"That's just awful."

Now he comes, his walk, his scent. "What's this, what's this, Bill?" That's what the mister says whenever he finds something dug up, or catches Bill on the furniture. I didn't dig, he thinks. I'm too weak. The man gets down and is touching him, scratching but very lightly, as though afraid. Where was he? Why was he gone?

He doesn't remember much of it, just the mister himself. No bitterness or silent treatment comes into play, no payback, none of the devices that would figure at such a moment, were Bill human. Hardly able to stand, what he experiences now is, in human terms, a simple sense of recovered congruity, of order restored. And the child. She is there now, at the mister's side, looking at him. He knows nothing of her, doesn't remember her lying on the carpet with him. But she shares something of the mister's scent. She is part of him, and therefore *heaven*.

"I suppose it's crazy," Glenda says. "I just couldn't leave him there. I knew when I left the house it was a mistake. 'Don't go, Glenda,' I told myself. 'Go down there and you'll be sorry.'" As Fred sits stroking the dog, Glenda explains about the bowls. What the hell—she tells him about the home videos. She is confessing to him, sharing her tormented self, hoping for an ally.

"I don't think you're crazy at all," he says. "What else is there? Who knows what goes on with them?"

Ruby kneels with the soles of her feet under her butt, hands on her knees. "You can smell the medicine," she says.

"It's become very important to me," Glenda says. "Too important. I know it has to do with Cliff. With Hotsie, too. That really is crazy, but it's true. Fred got him one of these microchips they put under the skin. When they called, it was like I had failed everything."

They stay an hour. Back at the house, he makes them tuna-and-cheese melts, one of her favorites. "He liked these," she says looking at her half-eaten sandwich. "I remember."

"He liked everything." His own sandwich tastes bad to him. He can still smell the dog.

"He didn't like corn."

"Neither do you." She smiles at him. "I see, I get it," he tells her. "He was your cleaner-upper under the table."

"Just corn. And liver. But he ate that."

"We've never had liver when you're with us."

"Once," she says. "Could we go back?"

"Home? We just got here, sweetie. In a few days."

"I mean to Bill's."

He watches her drinking her Coke. For some reason he can't remember, she and her brother aren't supposed to drink carbonated beverages. Letting Ruby have a soda represents one of several small conspiracies they enter into. They subvert what he sometimes thinks of as the well-intentioned but overly protective policies of both the kids' parents. Everything seems so dangerous to them. His grandchildren wear helmets for everything. Bikes, Razor Scooters. Every time they go in the pool, they have to shower. So much information on the hazards of just *being* has entered the public domain. Near the end of his own life, it seems to him that childhood has been turned into a no-man's land littered with biochemical land mines.

"Sure," he says. "Why not?"

"Right now?"

"Well, sweetie, I imagine Glenda has things to do."

"She said any time. She said she wanted us to come."

He knows what Ruby is thinking: If we go, he'll get better. He actually thinks Glenda might believe the same thing. He sees her opening the door, grabbing him. She's always been just a little over-the-top. But you can explain that in terms of being anxious to please in a place where she is viewed with suspicion and contempt. Today, though, she looked, well, crazy doesn't seem far off the mark.

As for Bill's getting better, it doesn't seem likely. The dog has too little left. As they were sitting with him, he lost control. A really awful, sick-smelling urine spread out from his hind quarters. Glenda cleaned it up, talking in the soothing way an especially decent nurse might treat a terminally ill patient.

Half an hour later when she answers the door, her face lights up. You're with me, it says. You know I'm nuts but you've hired on. She can't know his own feelings of guilt and anger at seeing something he loved so reduced, drained. The simple truth is, Bill meant more to Vinyl than he realized. The dog's vitality, his loyalty and trust had worked like an antidote for *Time*, the daily paper, the evening news. Seeing his dog on the floor, he felt ashamed. Responsible. You saved something and then threw it away, he thought.

When the two of them walk back to the dog, Ruby is already there. She is kneeling again, unwrapping the other half of her tuna melt. She breaks it in small pieces in her hand. Then—always a neat child—she puts the pieces on the paper towel she brought it in, saying nothing. She pushes the towel in front of the dog and sits back.

"I never thought of it," Glenda says. "I never thought of tuna. Hotsie loved it."

"He's eating—" Hands in fists on her knees, Ruby is rocking slightly. "He likes tuna fish."

"Why haven't you called?"

"Why haven't you? It works in both directions."

"Because you do," she says. "You go down to check on things and call."

"Well, I didn't, all right?"

His wife can hardly miss the edge in his voice. He wants to pin the rap on her. None of this would've happened if she hadn't gotten all bent out of shape about nothing. The dog wouldn't hurt anyone.

"How's Ruby?"

"Good."

"Good how? Give me details. Have you been anywhere? How's she eating?"

Why do all women believe everything can be understood in terms of food? "She's eating fine," he says. "We've had pizza, toaster waffles, tuna melts. How's that?" He tries to control his anger. Be fair, he thinks. If his wife never really liked Bill, she didn't hate the dog. One day you just sprang him on her, he thinks. Showed up and said, Meet Bill, our new family member.

"Well, all right, then. Is she there?"

"At the club. They have a summer program."

"You're kidding. Since when? What kind of program?"

"Some kid thing for grandchildren. Lesley Rauch told me about it." She is very good at catching him in small lies or half-truths, but this is the story he has decided to use. The odds improve when he gives details, so he adds, "Something to do with crafts. Pottery, I think."

"Ruby would love that," his wife says. "I'm surprised. I don't remember anything in the newsletter."

"Lesley said it was spur-of-the-moment." He wants to get off the topic. On it much longer, and he will screw up. "Listen, honey, I need to keep the line open. The cable's out. I don't want to face too many more hours without the Cartoon Network. I'll call tomorrow."

She says goodbye. He hangs up, making a mental note to cook up more specifics related to the spur-of-the-moment summer program for grandchildren. "The cable's out" he thinks was inspired. He doesn't mind telling his wife about Bill. But what he really won't be able to sit still for is a sarcastic monolog about Glenda, or interrogation about his visits there. He saw the incense sticks and empty liquor bottles, not to mention Glenda herself. All those dishes, he thinks. Home videos. If she weren't both a good person *and* desperate, she wouldn't be doing any of it.

Probably Bill would make it now anyway. He is getting large doses of a drug to counteract the poison in his blood stream. His ears are responding to the lotion, he is passing the parasites. Glenda refuses to believe it's the medicine. She *knows* the return of his owner and Ruby have tipped the scales. "You've made the difference," she keeps saying. "You and Ruby."

The girl asks if she can stay. She is on the floor with the dog and looks up at Glenda. He sees they worked this out when he was at the house lying about pottery classes and cable failure. He really *does* now feel committed, involved. He lets her stay, goes back home and sleeps well.

At Glenda's, a landmark moment comes that night when Bill

stands. It's after dinner. By now, the area around his cage is bunkered with plates heaped with flaked tuna. For good measure, Glenda also opened sardines and a can of mackerel in tomato sauce. And slices of both Gouda and New York Extra Sharp Cheddar. Then she made spaghetti for herself and Ruby. It's one of the few things she feels confident serving to others.

"Cliff did most of the cooking," she says. "He was good at it. As you can tell, I'm a shitty cook." She looks at Ruby across from her at the butcher-block table in the kitchen. "I'm sorry," Glenda says. "That just slipped out."

"It's okay."

"I apologize. Models don't always watch their mouths."

"Are you a model?"

"Was. That's how I met Cliff. You know what Lands' End is? A catalog company. They make sports clothes, bathing suits. I modeled for them. I had a lot of work because of the baby boomers. You know, looking good even though you're not so young anymore? That's what they wanted me for. We were here doing a shoot for the catalog. This guy with a dog kept throwing a Frisbee. It was really amazing, I'm telling you. Did you know Hotspur?"

"Was he a border collie?"

Glenda holds her fork poised before her mouth. She smiles, wearing her yoga leotard. "Why the fuck does that make me feel happy? Oh God—" Hand over her mouth, she shakes her head.

"My dad says that," Ruby tells her. "After he talks to my mom on the phone. They're divorced."

Glenda takes her hand away, still shaking her head. "I don't know anything about kids," she says. "I never had a child. Please don't tell your grandfather, okay?" Ruby promises. "Where was I?"

"On the beach. You saw a man with a dog."

"Right, thank you. Well, Ruby, you had to be there. We had maybe I think it was seven models and three cameramen. Plus makeup and all that. We're on the beach—you know, you see it on TV. Running on the beach, in the surf acting super life-is-great. They tell you just that kind of thing— 'More life-is-great, Glenda, more I-can't-get-enough-of this—' Anyway, this dog, Ruby—I don't know how else to say it. He rounded us up. He corralled all of us between the sailboards we had for props, and the changing cabanas. You should've seen it."

There's been no one to tell this or anything else to. Cliff died and was cremated, but it wasn't the end of anything. Now, Glenda pours out her heart, slipping several times with bad words, apologizing. Opening a bottle of wine, she tells how, that day, Cliff had come and gotten Hotspur. "The dog really hit on me," she says. "If you want the truth, the dog was the first thing. You know these ads, some super macho stud holding a baby? I later told Cliff it was sort of like that. You know, sort of flattering him."

When they finish the spaghetti, she goes to the refrigerator and looks in. In the crisper she finds wrinkled apples, some unappetizing-looking grapes. She closes the door and opens the freezer compartment. Eclairs, purchased in the shopping trip to Publix that Cliff made the morning he died, rest on a bag of his hash browns. Glenda ponders the foggy interior. She's kept everything from that trip, unwilling to use Cliff up. With Ruby, the moment has come. She gets out the eclairs and puts them on plates.

When the girl comes back at two, Glenda is doing yoga.

Bill is eating. If a dog with such big jaws could be said to nibble, that's what he's doing with flaked tuna. But when he drinks water, the sound is exactly the same as Ruby remembers— a big-dog sloshing, lapping sound, water splashing on the floor. Done, Bill turns away and steps slowly to the glass doorwall. He doesn't sit, just stands looking out. She remembers how he sat and looked out at grandpa's, so alert. Vigilant, grandpa called it. Now he is just looking, like someone in front of a fish aquarium thinking something else.

She goes to him and rests her hand on his back. "I think he should go out," she says. Reflected in the glass, Glenda sits in the lotus position. Eyes closed, palms up on her knees, she nods. Ruby pulls on the doorwall and slides it past Bill. His nose works. His ears. Several seconds pass, but she can see he recognizes the change. Now he steps down onto the cement deck.

Ruby doesn't follow. What if he gives up and comes back in? The sultry air coming through the opening worries her. Her grandparents talk about people dying of heatstroke in houses where the air conditioning failed. Her father used a word, hyposomething, reading about street people in New York who died from the cold. Bill is so weak and thin, moving like the sick horse in—she can't remember the movie's name. Any little thing that burdens his body might do it. It's wrong, she thinks. You made a mistake. Germs grow everywhere in weather like this.

"Bill—" She watches him moving around the end of the oval pool. On the far side he stops and looks out. Her heart is pounding. She has done the wrong thing again, failed. Now the dog will die. Germs, heat. Another storm, she thinks. What if he has a heart attack? Dad won't scold her this time, but she'll know. What if he has an attack like Mr. Gilmore? Glenda has told her about it. They were playing Frisbee, she said. Those are his ashes—she pointed to a vase thing on the stand next to her big TV. Please don't tell your grandparents. I had Hotsie cremated, too. He's in the box. Promise, Ruby. It's really crazy, how do I know what's in there? But that might be true for Cliff. Don't tell, okay?

Since the time the baby fell, whenever they ask her to watch it, rock it, hold the baby for more digital pictures to send on the computer to dad wherever he's working—she remembers. And it will always be that way, every morning when she gets up, every afternoon when she comes back from some stupid new school—

Glenda is standing next to her. Bill sits before the screen cage, facing the eleventh fairway. "God, he's noble," Glenda says.

"We should make him come in."

"He'll know when. He really is noble. Even in bad shape, he looks..."

Ruby looks back at the dog. "Handsome," she says.

"Handsome. You're right." Glenda nods. "Ruggedly handsome. Taking in his kingdom. Hotsie used to sit out there just like that. Just checking it out, like a general."

"Like a security guard."

"No, not some poor flunky in a mall. Like an admiral."

"Or a cowboy looking over his ranch," Ruby says. "Or a head waiter." Glenda laughs. "That's what grandpa says he looks like."

* * * *

Beyond having done a good job of reading the needs and anticipating the questions of vinyl siding customers, Ruby's grandfather has never thought of himself as having good people skills. He knows enough to avoid political subjects with his more opinionated golf partners, he can tell a joke. But even after all this time—what? forty-four years next February—he still gets things wrong often enough with the missus.

Letting Ruby stay nights at Glenda Gilmore's represents a significant decision. He knows what his wife would say. He considers her smarter than himself in most things. But he sticks with his decision. When he walks along the back path and looks, the two are in the living room, talking. Glenda's showing Ruby yoga. Ruby is washing windows the second time he passes, talking behind the glass and not seeing him until he waves. She waves back, but doesn't open the doorwall either time. What's going on inside belongs to her. He's smart enough to see it, and keeps going.

The degree of his confidence in the decision manifests itself each time he speaks to his wife. Failing so often to successfully bend or sidestep the truth with her, he long ago gave up trying. Not now. "You're going to be impressed," he tells her. "I know I am. I think she has talent, I went up and watched yesterday. The woman they have running the class came over. You know when someone's just being polite or encouraging. There was none of that."

"I wish I was there. Are you taking pictures?"

He winces. "She says it distracts them. She asked everyone to hold off until the exhibition."

"Oh, I wish I was there. What's Ruby making?"

He's ready for this. "Horses and dogs. I think maybe she and Ronald should have a puppy."

"Well, the yard at the new house is supposed to be fenced. Tell me who else has kids down." He names three people they aren't close to and invents others, anonymous renters, to fill out the "class." "I thought the Kriegers were in Massachusetts."

He's ready for this, too. "The storm. Larry was watching on the Weather Channel. He just wanted to be sure."

"How I wish I was there. I miss you."

"I miss you, too."

"I miss you more." She always says this when they're separated.

"Guess what? The Babbitts had to sell the house in Minnesota. The boat, too. They're still here."

"Uh oh. You always thought they were over-extended." Good. He's relieved to move on from fiction to hard news. It doesn't last long. "All right, then," she says. "But Fred, I really do want to speak to her on the next call. What time does she go to the club?"

Make it late, he thinks. Give yourself time for rehearsal. "Nine."

"Good. Call at breakfast, before you take her up."

He walks the path, already sweating as he nears the Gilmores'. He loves Naples. For him, wintering here represents perfection. But he leaves willingly in June. The only good thing about Naples in the summer comes from something missing—thousands of snowbirds like himself. Without them, road congestion disappears, restaurant hostesses practically fall at your feet, tradesmen actually show up when they should. Otherwise, the sauna atmosphere is oppressive.

When he stops at the back of the cage, Bill is looking out. He sees Vinyl and barks. It heartens him. He goes to the screen door and lets himself in. Hearing the dog, he moves to the slider. Glenda is unwinding from her yoga mat. Ruby's on the floor, too, with her knitting. As the slider rolls open Bill barks again but now smells him. He lowers his head and comes to what was once the source of all good things. Vinyl bends and holds the dog's head. He scratches his neck. "You look a little better, old scout," he says. "Old timer."

He eats lunch with them, Bill on the floor next to him. Peanut butter sandwiches and blender smoothies Glenda makes with frozen fruit. He lets them do the talking. Bill's been walking around the house, Glenda tells him. Just now? That was his first bark. He whined this morning to be let out. For the first time, the dog peed on the deck, not in the house. "And he pooped," Ruby says, something that must be of special importance to grownups, owing to the canisters of Metamusil at her grandparents', and detailed discussions about the new baby's "production."

"If you could stay with Bill for about an hour, we need to do some grocery shopping," Glenda says. She is rinsing dishes at the sink. "We made a list."

"Could you go alone? I need to talk to Ruby." Glenda looks over her shoulder at him. She seems fearful. "Just until you get back," he says. "Bill needs his regular team and I have some chores." Reassured, she nods and turns back. "You know, Ruby could be washing those," he says.

"Ruby cleaned the bathroom. She did an ace job, as Cliff would say. She helped me wash down Bill's area when he was on the deck. We're getting this place shipshape."

After she leaves, the two sit on the floor. Glenda has moved the coffee table away from the sectional sofa. Bill's crate now occupies the space. "It's there if he wants it," Ruby explains. "Glenda thinks it gives him security. But he mostly sleeps on the rug."

A Midwesterner in mind and spirit, Ruby's grandfather doesn't like lies. Not that Midwesterners don't lie with the best of them. They just tend to live where conventional notions still persist. When they lie, they feel guilty. It's wrong and they know it. That's why his wife always catches him at it.

"I've done something I'm not proud of," he says. "I made up a story about you taking a pottery class down here. It's hard to explain. It has to do with Glenda."

"You did it because Grandma hates her," Ruby says. "She told me all the ladies think she hits on their husbands. They think she just married Cliff for his money, but she didn't. I mean she did, she said they weren't totally wrong about that. She didn't think she would've married him if he was poor. But she says that wasn't the biggest reason. And she never went cruising for other action."

A lot has been going on here in the old Pottery Barn, he thinks. "Grandma doesn't hate her," he says. "I don't think she hates anyone. It mostly has to do with Glenda being young."

"And because she still has her figure and was a model," Ruby says. He sees she has started a new scarf. This one's orange, a color he now notices in the drapes, and the sectional couch. "What's wrong with being a model?" she asks.

"I have no idea. No, I guess I do. Some people think making money off your looks is tacky. They think models aren't smart."

"Bimbos."

"Yes. I happen to think they're being dishonest," he says, watching Ruby knit. "Models just sell things. That's pretty much what everyone is doing all the time anyway. In one way or another."

"What about me?"

A delicate moment. He doesn't want to break their bond, but sees a chance to make a point. "I would say you're the buyer," he says. "A certain person is trying to sell herself, but you keep saying no." That's enough, he thinks. Don't push. "Back to the pottery class," he says. "I didn't want grandma to know you were staying here. Or about Bill. I said you were in this class making pottery horses and dogs. She wants to talk to you tomorrow at breakfast."

"And we should get our story straight."

Ten years old, he thinks. She knows too much already. "All right, yes."

"When I'm at mom's and dad calls, we do it all the time."

"I don't want to know. And promise not to tell Glenda," he adds, hearing himself, then seeing himself in free-fall down a moral slippery slope.

When Glenda returns, Vinyl walks back to his house. He sets about repairing the screen door Bill has torn. His granddaughter helps Glenda put away the groceries. She resumes her knitting, sitting next to Bill who now and then eats from one of the bowls. Glenda repositions her mat and begins stretching exercises. "Isn't that boring after a while?" Ruby asks.

"Only if you're doing something wrong." Glenda has always been supple and wants to stay that way. Stretching, she watches Ruby's flying fingers. The girl is seated cross-legged, her right hip touching Bill's side. He's going to make it, she thinks.

"Would your folks let you have a dog?" she asks. "I think it would be good."

"They're afraid because of the baby."

Glenda stands on one foot and assumes the tree pose. After a minute, she extends herself in the warrior pose. "People with dogs," she says. "They don't all give them away when they have a baby." Or, maybe they do, she has no idea. Friends in the business own little dogs, like the ones here. They take them on assignments. Sleep with them, make decisions about boyfriends based on the dog's response. She believes some of them would first give up the father *or* the baby. In the three days here, Ruby has done a lot of talking. About teachers, about school friends in Brooklyn Heights she won't see now except weekends, about her brother who can swim and run better than she can, but who is just knitting because she does. She is close to her mother, the administrative assistant for "someone big" at an ad agency. Even though she travels a lot and has boyfriends, the mother hasn't fallen out of favor. But Ruby adores her father. She shows Glenda wallet photos taken at the lake in Michigan. "He can't ski very well," she says. "He says trying is the important thing."

"You should work on them about a dog," Glenda says.

"I think we should take Bill for a walk." Ruby gets up. "We can try it, and if he gets tired we'll come back."

Glenda finishes her exercises. She goes in the bedroom and changes into conservative golf shorts and a baggy camp shirt, clothes that will keep anyone looking through a window from foaming at the mouth. She gets Hotspur's lead and fastens it to Bill's collar. "What do you think?" she says. "Are you ready?" Maybe not. He stays flat on the floor. She drops the lead and moves to the foyer where Ruby is waiting. When she opens the door, he looks slowly left. Right. He's looking for Fred, she thinks. He wants his master. But now Bill stands. He shakes himself with weak-legged, old-dog slowness, and then walks toward them. No running or dancing, but he comes.

"I knew this Japanese model. We were in Hawaii, we shared a room. She set up this little altar on the writing table. I asked about it, she said it honored her ancestors and the emperor. I always wondered about all that stuff with an emperor. I thought he was like a king. No, she said. More like a god. I asked was the emperor immortal, she said just his soul. But don't you believe everyone has one? She says, his soul is the soul of the Japanese people. He unites us. Everyone's loyal to the emperor, not just to themselves. Don't you think that's interesting?"

Is Ruby thinking about it, or something else? They are walking slowly, Bill between them. He steps now off the pavement, to a lamppost. Glenda follows, holding the lead. He sniffs then squats instead of raising his leg. It moves her out of all proportion.

"I thought about that story a lot," Glenda says, waiting for him to finish. "Especially since Cliff died. Hotspur was like our emperor. He united us. We cared about Hotsie together and it worked sort of the same way." She laughs, wiping her eyes but amused, too. "That's something else don't tell your grandpa."

"We studied Greeks last year," Ruby says. "All the gods and goddesses."

"You'll have to tell me. I don't know any of that."

As they resume the walk, men ahead are coming from a house. Their truck stands at the curb. Flexing between them, boards of some kind sway with their movements. "That's Lydia Stafford's house," Glenda says. "Do you know her?"

"No."

"She was always decent to me." Reaching the workers, she asks after the owner. She has moved, they don't know where. The work order calls for them to take up the flooring, all of it Dade County pine and cypress. They are to truck it to an address in Palm Beach. She thanks them and looks down at Bill. Head now lowered, he is panting. "Let's go back," she says. Walking again, Glenda shakes her head. "I didn't even know. I wonder when she left. She had a dog, a poodle."

"Brown?"

"That's it. Cliff said it was a very smart dog. Everyone here calls the owner Madame. That was her husband's name for her, before he died. I think she liked me because she didn't feel very plugged in here, either," Glenda says, remembering. "You know, not connected. She stopped playing golf after her husband died. She only played it for him, she didn't like the game. Didn't play cards. *Hated* mah-jongg, she said. I always felt like I let her down. We'd meet her with Hotspur, she'd be out with Emma I think was the name. She'd tell us about the book she was reading. I'm not much of a reader, so I never knew it."

At bedtime, Glenda sets the alarm. The next morning at eight, Ruby goes up the block to her grandfather's. They get their story straight, then call. Fred uses the cordless, Ruby the wall phone in the kitchen. "I hear you're quite the potter," her grandmother says.

"Horses and dogs."

"And alligators." It's one of the extra details they decided on. "And geckos. You put them in this kiln to bake. Now we're studying glazes." Ruby knows the terms from a unit at school. Last winter, everyone fired clay projects.

"Glazes." Her grandmother clucks. "I'm impressed."

"Madame left," Fred tells her. "I checked with administration. She's in assisted living, Terracina Grande."

"You should go see her."

"Of course I will."

"It's just there, isn't it?" she says. "Fate. Genes. It's selfish, but I hear a story like that and always wonder if I'm next."

"You're fine," he says, realizing from his wife's unguarded comment that she has for the moment forgotten Ruby is on the line. For one second it frightens him. She never forgets such things. "Listen, you two talk," he says. "Too much coffee, I have to go to the john." He puts down the cordless, feeling ashamed. You don't have to go to the can, he thinks. You're leaving Ruby to do all the dirty work. If she doesn't slip up about Bill and Glenda, he prefers to think their deception will serve some purpose. Either way, he still believes in his decision.

* * * *

Whenever he now comes along the back of the Gilmore house or rings the bell, it is painfully apparent the dog still regards him as his master. After all that's happened, Bill still honors him above all others. He struggles up more quickly, moves with greater purpose over the slippery floor, nails clicking. Reaching the man, he lowers his head, deferring to the alpha as he waits to be scratched.

But Fred doesn't go often. He visits Lydia Stafford—Madame—in her new assisted-living apartment. By turns her old self, then vague, he sees she has developed a strategy for buying time until able to place visitors. She seems cheerful enough, chatty and witty as he remembers her. It had to be hard for her these years alone without Archie. A refined, well-read woman among golfers, he thinks. He waits apprehensively for her to bring up Emma. When she doesn't he feels relieved.

Back home, he takes up chores. He goes to Home Depot and comes back with more shelving for the spare bedroom's walk-in closet. He also needs more shelving in the garage, but it's too hot. When Glenda calls to ask if he wants to come walking with them, he begs off with something that needs doing—more small lies. Then he stands at the front window and watches them pass. The lead is gone. When Ruby stops, Bill sits. When she gives the command and gesture, he walks forward or stays until called. Ruby is teaching Bill's new mistress how it's done.

Glenda wants to save the dog whatever fear might come from a visit to the vet's. Miraculously, she finds one that makes house calls. Before he comes, she and Ruby get a urine sample—"Don't ask us how," Glenda says—and a stool sample. The vet uses her stethoscope, looks in Bill's mouth and ears, checks his paws, draws blood. The following day, she declares Bill officially "on the mend."

And it's time to go. Ruby has talked several times to her mother, her father and stepmother. Does he just want to hear it, or has she actually shown some small evidence of thaw, a brief but real moment of spontaneity in speaking to her stepmom?

Listening on the cordless as Ruby goes on with what are now the highly detailed particulars of her pottery class, he looks forward to getting back.

Glenda pulls to a stop in the lot opposite Terminal B. They are flying Spirit. Next to her, Fred is looking down and talking to Bill, scratching him behind the ears. The dog is on the floor between the Explorer's two captain's chairs. Now she looks in the rearview. Ruby has loosened her seatbelt to stroke the dog's hindquarters. Glenda dreamed two nights ago of the dog standing over her on the bed, wanting to know where his master and Ruby had gone. Their leaving makes her feel vulnerable.

Get a grip, she thinks. When Ruby looks up at the rearview, Glenda smiles. "I think your granddad and I will give you and Bill a minute to say goodbye." She loosens her belt and gets out. Fred does the same. As he comes around the front of her SUV, a Northwest plane is hissing in takeoff. What a nice old guy, she thinks. No Cliff, but that isn't fair. And Ruby. If she has ever experienced maternal feelings, Glenda can't remember. She isn't all that sure her feelings for Ruby could be called that. Sisters, she thinks. Maybe that's why we get along well.

"I'm going to break a promise," she says facing the terminal. "I wouldn't if I didn't think you should know."

"There's been a fair amount of that on this trip," he says.

"We were talking. I shouldn't have, but I'd had some wine. I was telling her how when Cliff and I first started seeing each other, I was living with this guy. I didn't tell him about Cliff. It was cowardly. I picked some fight to break it off. Accused him of cheating, completely bogus. It's not a thing to tell a little girl, what can I say? It just came out. She says, 'I did that with Bill. I blamed him like that, and they took him to the shelter.' I didn't push it, but I think it had to do with your new grandson."

Fred smiles, looking into the Florida midday sky. "It's all right.

I think I knew something like that happened. It could easily have happened. He really is big."

"Anyway, that's what Ruby said. It was a big deal to her. She saved it a long time."

"She's a great girl."

"I know how your wife feels, but please let me see Ruby when you're down."

He looks to her. When he takes his hands from his pockets Glenda embraces him. After a long moment, he steps back and holds her forearms. "Absolutely," he says. "My wife's not a mean person. We'll come see you and Bill, you'll come see us."

The New World Order

On the ground at Metro Airport, the two move through the tunnel. A tradition of greeting or being greeted at airports figures between Fred and his wife. Like other long-standing habits it goes unnoticed, but is forty years old.

Security no longer permits such moments in boarding lounges. Ruby and her grandfather walk quickly with others toward the escalator leading down to the baggage claim. Along with his carry-on, Fred lugs a sack of pink grapefruit, another tradition. Ruby's small red Pokemon suitcase flaps at her side. She explained on the way down how it also serves as her school book bag. What happened to backpacks? he asked. This is how we do it now, grandpa, she said. Both she and Ronald have tried to explain the intricacies of Pokemon to him, the many characters' special powers and vulnerabilities, what they're compatible with or attacked by. He couldn't get it.

In her other hand she holds a plastic bag wrapped around a small ceramic horse. The horse is for grandma, to serve as corroborating evidence of the summer class. Part of the bottom is missing ("I dropped it in the airport bathroom"), where *Made in China* was stamped. He feels frustrated to still be dreaming up untruths. Then why are you? he wonders. What he said to Glenda is true. His wife is generous. Tolerant, thoughtful. She has her blind spots, but who doesn't?

"Which airport?" Ruby asks, matching her stride to his.

"What, sweetie? This is Detroit Metropolitan Airport. Grandma's going to pick us up and drive us home."

"No. Which airport did I drop it?" Ruby holds up the plastic.

"Fort Myers. On the tile floor, that's why it chipped."

Blind spots. For instance, corrupting children. But he doesn't really believe it. The conspiracy has added to the value of whatever took place in Naples. The truth of it early on led him to view the spur-of-the-moment decision for his granddaughter to fly down with him as a gift. A blessing. He feels confident something positive has happened for both Ruby and Glenda, he can't say what. For you, too, he thinks. Doing something for the dog has redeemed him a bit.

They start down. As the moving stairs edge lower, his wife appears—expectant, smiling. He's never been more grateful to see her. In the moment, the strength of his gratitude surprises, almost alarms him. He cannot imagine coming back, riding the stairs this way, and not seeing her. It will happen, he thinks. To one of us, pretty soon. But not yet.

Hugs and questions about the flight, weather. After the fashion of all bad actors, Ruby promptly gets her scene underway with too much build. "The class was really neat," she says. "All the stuff I made is at the house except this—" She hands up the evidence.

"Well, thank you." They decided on this as a way to buy time before eventually telling the truth. As his wife with due ceremony unwraps the plastic, he thinks how lucky it is for them, for the whole country, that he went into vinyl siding and not counter-intelligence. His wife holds up the horse. However little the person in China was paid to make it, the ceramic piece still displays a level of craftsmanship remarkable for a ten-year-old.

"This is amazing, Ruby," his wife says. "So lifelike. So real."

"Remember I told about learning glazes?"

"You most certainly did learn *something*," she says, glancing from horse to husband. She turns it in her hands.

"It fell," Ruby explains. "In the Metro airport."

"Here?"

"I mean the one down there. In Florida."

"It's beautiful, Ruby. Thank you."

By the time they reach Ann Arbor, everything is already unraveling. By Flint, Fred and Ruby surrender. "I see," his wife says. "That's very elaborate. You must both think I'm very small-minded."

"No, Grandma, we don't. You just don't know her, is all. Glenda was a model. She told me that's why other ladies don't like her. Because they think it means she's a gold digger, but she's not. She showed me yoga. I showed her how to walk Bill with the commands. She didn't know what they were, Cliff never took Hotspur to school. Hotspur was always on the lead. Now her and Bill walk the way I used to walk him. After his first wife died, he just wanted a dog to hang out with and be company. His second wife didn't work out, she was gone in six months. Then he met Glenda at the beach, she was down for a shoot for Lands' End—"

His wife has the horse in her hands and is looking straight ahead. Fred has the advantage of driving. In tight situations, driving can work for you something like knitting. You're busy, people's lives are in your hands. The monolog continues—intense, detailed. And because his wife is not finally small-minded, she hears in all this the why behind what happened down in Florida.

* * * *

September arrives. Ruby and Ronald move with their parents into the new house. They like the change of school better than either of them wants to admit. Still seeing friends on weekends, neither of them really misses the old one, the car- and truck-glutted streets and litter surrounding it in Brooklyn Heights. In the manner of children, they come home announcing new allegiances and attachments that have formed overnight. When Ruby tells her parents about the Florida trip, her stepmother reveals that several of her law firm's clients are top models. She even writes a thank-you note to Glenda Gilmore, showing it to Ruby for her approval, adding at her request the part about the horse.

Other things—a growing interest in the new baby—begin to ease the logjam separating Ruby and her stepmother. Now, though, Ronald begins showing signs of rebellion, particularly after weekends in the city. He's always been closer than his sister to their mother. Her pet, her little man. "It's day to day," the stepmother says on the phone. "We all have our moments."

Wisely, she agrees to let them have a dog. When the children call with the news, Ruby asks what kind of dog Bill is. "A Lab mix," her grandfather says. "A mutt." The stepmother comes on. "Labradors are even-tempered," he tells her. "But I know your concerns about big dogs." The kids ask around at school, their parents quiz colleagues at work. Whatever you do, people say, do *not* go near a pet store. Most puppies in stores have been bred in puppy mills. What you get can't be predicted. Visiting shelters and breeders with their father and stepmother, Ruby and Ronald can't decide. "They want them all," their father says. "Who wouldn't? Puppies are not fair." When a dog owned by the cousin of a girl on the same block whelps her second litter, Ruby and Ronald bring home a new Shetland sheep dog, a male. Ruby names him Emperor.

He catches a lot of smallmouth. He and the missus play golf and gin rummy with friends. In the third week of September, neighbors from their old community north of Detroit come to visit for four days. They all drive to Chicago and see a new production of *Crazy for You*. The music holds up for them. The two couples bob their heads, getting into the tap dancing. Home, Fred paints the two bedrooms in the guest cabin. He rakes leaves, puts down fresh sealer on the floor of the screened porch. In the first week of October, the crew drags out the pontoon boat.

He comes in at four and washes his hands at the sink. Oprah is playing on the set in the cavernous great room. He steps in using the hand towel. "Want a rob roy?"

His wife looks at her watch. "Pretty early."

"This is true. Tea?"

"I got a call from Glenda Gilmore. She wants you to call her back. The number's on the pad. Tea would be good."

"Did she say what it's about?"

His wife uses the remote's mute button and looks over. "You remember they grandfathered Bill because there was no bylaw on dog size? They added a ruling last year. Twenty-four inches maximum."

"I remember. They had to make an exception."

"For us, not her. They say he left and came back, so the current rule now applies to him. I think she wants your advice on housing. Call her and see."

"How'd she sound?"

"Good. Mad about being hassled, but she sounded in charge. She's thinking of going back to work. Go talk to her."

He walks back to the kitchen. It irritates him, the pettiness of club regulations. They have rules for everything. How to put out your trash, what kinds of clothes to wear. You can wear shorts in the grill room, not in the dining room three steps down. No one allowed on the course wearing a shirt without a collar. No liquor or wine bottles except clear ones in the recycling bin. Actually, he believes in such rules. They make for order and contribute to civility, but you can carry them too far.

He taps the number. Glenda answers. "Hi," she says. "Your wife told you?"

"I'm sorry, Glenda. It's pretty picky."

"He's right here. I bet he knows you're on the line, don't you?"

"How's he doing?"

"Maybe not what he was. You'd know better than me. But he's good. I guess, though, I'm going to have to lease or sell this place and find something else. You've been down here and know a lot, I just thought you might have some suggestions."

He gives her the names of two realtors he knows to be reliable. "Your best bet is probably a house in one of the single-family communities," he says. "Kids, dogs. Some place you can do your own thing without a lot of micromanaging. I hear you're going back to work."

"I got some calls, there's work. I don't really need to, but I'm starting to think it makes sense. Here or Fort Myers. Or Sarasota. Nowhere out of state," she says. "Now that I have family to think of. How's my goddaughter?"

That's what Glenda has started calling Ruby in her calls to report on Bill's progress. She also phoned Ruby. He tells Glenda things are better with Ruby, and that he's convinced Glenda deserves some of the credit. "Bill does, too," she says. "Everybody feels better being useful." When he tells her about the Shetland puppy, Glenda says, "Now *that's* news."

Two days later on the second Wednesday in October, he hears the shop vac out in the garage. He opens the door from the kitchen. His wife is vacuuming the van. She looks intent, almost grim. He always vacuums at the car wash, but when she gets ideas it's best to leave her alone. At dinner, they share a bottle of good Rhone wine, but she remains thoughtful and quiet. Later, watching *Law and Order*, she says, "Let's go down early."

"It's not even November."

"You can get the dock taken out. I called, they're available."

"What's the deal? Why all of a sudden?"

"We're done with chores here. Why hang around?"

Well, okay. He doesn't get it, but if she wants to leave, they'll leave. The next day she packs and he gets an oil change. They load the van Saturday night. She is still being squirrelly with him. Strange. Sometimes, he has the impression she's mad, other times not. But when they go to bed, she rolls to him and makes it clear what they're going to do. He takes a pill, and soon they make love as they have for years now. He doesn't know whether the sameness represents the final product after various prototypes, or just a loss of need for novelty. Either way, the best part these days is lying together after, having proved they are still up to it.

"You never give me enough credit," she says.

"Sure I do."

"I never disliked Glenda Gilmore."

Sure you did, he thinks, holding his wife close. It's only taken forty years, but he now knows somewhat better when and when not to speak. Over time, peace has become far more important than being right.

"If you guys ever went through what we do, you might understand," she says.

"I'm sure that's true."

"You drink all that beer, all those rob roys. Nothing happens to you, you have different metabolisms. But I could've been more friendly," she says. "A better neighbor. She moves in with all us old people. It had to be hard." He holds her closer, to show he appreciates what she means. He doesn't, but that's not the point.

"And I never disliked Bill," she says. This he finds much more difficult not to answer, but manages with just a sigh. "You just sprang him on me," she tells him. "Out of nowhere. A big decision like that. A big dog. I should have had some say."

"That's true."

"She really wants to go back to work. She's going crazy now, she told me. I'd like to know her better. Someone young for a change."

"The club will give her time to relocate," he says. "We'll have her to dinner. I'm sorry you didn't see her with Ruby."

"The pottery class."

"Right."

"You and your secrets."

The following day, they get an early start. At I-75, they turn south. This is the beginning of the grind, the tedious, unappealing stretch of road leading from flat southern Michigan through flat Ohio. This is the opening phase of the snowbirds' Chisholm Trail, the annual southbound roundup. Starting in late October, Conestoga wagons reinvented as thousands of minivans and SUVs begin rolling all one way, heading for the peninsula jutting down from Georgia like the boot of Italy.

They listen to books. All day, Elmore Leonard's *Riding the Rap* keeps them interested. Numbed by road vibration and the low-key anxiety of high-speed travel, they drive in two-hour shifts. They stop to fuel themselves and the van, stretch, buy coffee and soft drinks. They say little and listen to the book.

At night, they always stop north of Atlanta. When he leaves the expressway and asks if she wants a Marriott this time, she says, "What's wrong with the Red Roof Inn?"

"Nothing. We always stayed there because of Bill. I thought you might like something more upscale."

"The Red Roof is fine," she says.

They check in, wash their faces and change into clean polos, then drive to the casual restaurant they know from previous trips. A combination sports bar and roadhouse steak restaurant, its walls flash with dozens of TV screens. Green-shaded lamps hang over the booths. They are shown to one by the manager. Looking twelve to both of them, the boy-man wears a rep tie and dress shirt. It seems to Fred like a school uniform. His wife orders house chardonnay, he asks for a rob roy on the rocks.

When the drinks come, Fred holds up his glass. "A good day," he says. "We make a good team."

"We do." She clinks his glass. "So young," she says of the manager.

"How did it happen?" he asks. "I can't believe managers of anything ever looked like that. It adds a whole different angle to someone like Glenda."

"She won't stay," his wife says.

"Probably not."

"She's still young. Donegal is too old a crowd." Sipping her wine, she regards him. She puts the glass down, still looking at him, smiling now. "Oh hell, you keep your secrets," she says. "I'm no good at it. Bill's coming back."

"What are you talking about?"

"Glenda would keep him, of course. 'He's a great dog. He's no Hotspur but no dog could be—' That's what she said last week. We talked again, we *girls*. She says he stares out the window. She thinks he's looking for you."

"That's crazy." He hears the emphasis in his voice, for himself, not her. "That's what they do," he says. "He does it all the time."

"I know, but it's what she thinks. Plus, there's the 'grandfather' business. It applies to you but not to her. I called the club manager. I told him Glenda was just keeping Bill for us. I can tell a fib or two myself, you know."

"I see that."

He smiles at his wife. From what he knows of her after only forty-four years, he determines now, with some confidence, that everything's already been worked out. By the *girls*, he thinks. He sips his drink, hearing crowd sounds from the wall-mounted sets. Young men at the bar erupt, pounding the counter. He turns away, seeing himself at Glenda Gilmore's front door, the door opening. The damned thing can't stop leaping, scolding—Where *were* you! Why *went* you! How *could* you!—barking, leaping, big paws on his chest and the mister holding them, looking at the dog, delighted to be known, being told off but welcomed. *Okay okay, come on now—*

With special thanks to
Peg Goldberg Longstreth
and

Gold Mountain Press,

the author wishes to acknowledge the following people and dogs for contributions small and large to *Just Bill*: Evalene, Lorne, Doc, Harvey and Chelsea Knister; Georgia, Bob, and Shadow Nelson; Rick and Joyce McKissen, Sheila Fawcett, Ellie Rounds; Mark, Nancy, Clara and Ava Peeters; Betty Stover, Flo and Chrissie Gloeckner, Lew and Precious Biggs, Rebeca and Zoe Brown, Sandra and Tequila Critz; Jan Collins, DVM; Jack, Wanda and Maxwell Smart Mayo; Bill, Marylou and Mollie Grimes; Nancy and Duncan Hogan, Marcia and Jack Boettcher; Ed, Margaret, Bear and Courtney Carr; Frank, Joan, Lesley, Nina, Lola, Princess and Tinkerbell Rauch; Sanders, Nick and Ranger Wider; Tanqueray, Rosie and Brody Monkman; Lori and Buck Robins; Elizabeth, Rose, Wagner and Fricka Forest; Skippy Wilson, G'kar and Kira Lighton; Marshall, Liebe, Mollie and Murphy; Reesie and Frida Thompson, Don and Benji Frankenberger, Warren and Paddy Kirk; David, Shereen and Tootsie Willens; Jim, Liz and Taffy; Diesel, Henry and Odie Rist; along with those who have skipped my mind, the Vanderburgh Humane Society of Evansville, Indiana, and (with gratitude and admiration) Marjorie Cox and Cheri Melloy.